NORMAN FIRTH

KNIGHT-ERRANT

Complete and Unabridged

LINFORD
Leicester

First published in Great Britain

First Linford Edition
published 2018

A catalogue record for this book is available
from the British Library.

ISBN 978–1–4448–3730–8

Published by
F. A. Thorpe (Publishing)
Anstey, Leicestershire

Set by Words & Graphics Ltd.
Anstey, Leicestershire
Printed and bound in Great Britain by
T. J. International Ltd., Padstow, Cornwall

This book is printed on acid-free paper

KNIGHT-ERRANT

1

In Which We Meet a Lady in Distress

He first noticed her in Sylvester's Restaurant in the Strand, where he had gone for dinner. She was not young but certainly not old — she might have been anywhere between the ages of twenty-five and thirty — and she was beautiful.

She was beautiful in a dark, exotic way, and he wondered if she might be of foreign nationality. Whatever she was, she stood out among the other beautiful women there, like a butterfly against a crowd of moths. And in spite of the dark mystery of her, there was something about her that said clearly she was not of their type; that her life contained some deeper, subtler meaning than did the lives of the women about her with their new hats, new beauty specialists, and interminable cocktail parties.

He might not have noticed her at all

had it not been for the presence of the man with her. That man interested Lance Knight, for he was well-known in certain circles, and Lance Knight was interested in things happening within those same circles.

Yes, he was very much interested in the man called Sebastian Farlow,

Had you asked anyone who knew Lance Knight what he was and why he was, they'd have told you: 'Lance Knight? A damned interfering busybody!' They would have said that had they been police officials or crooks. And even if that sounds like a contradiction, it is nevertheless true.

Or they might have said: 'Lance Knight? Oh, yes, the fellow the newspapers call 'the Knight.' Yes, I know him a bit — I've read of him. He's independent — got plenty of money and nothing to do with it. Spends his time tracking down criminals outside the pale of the law. Useful chap to society.'

Or they might have said, if they were envious: 'He ought to do a real job of work — trouble is, he's afraid of it!' The self-righteous would have said that, ignoring the fact that had they had Lance Knight's fortune, they wouldn't even have striven to lift a hand for any purpose at all.

Lance was afraid of work; no one was more ready to admit it. The earlier part of his life in the slums, before a distant relative had died and left him seventy thousand pounds, had shown him what it meant to have to be dependent upon a cruel, avaricious taskmaster for your livelihood. He had worked hard then but had seen no future for himself in anything. Then had come the money; and here he was — man-about-town, thirty-two, dark, good-looking, with a bank balance anyone would have welcomed, and a habit of dabbling in all kinds of trouble no one would have welcomed.

He looked at Sebastian Farlow again, and his brow wrinkled very thoughtfully. Farlow wasn't very impressive; he ran to fat a lot, and he boasted three double chins, and a rather loud suit. His face was dark and greasy, his hair oiled back to his head to hide the bald spot on top. He might have been about fifty-one or two, and he was noted for his unscrupulous methods of getting anything he wanted.

Lance had for some time considered the idea of seeing what he could do about Farlow; he had made enquiries about the man, and unearthed one or two interesting facts that unfortunately could not be verified. But Lance knew they were true; he knew that the real man behind the erection of Gorsham super-cinema — which had collapsed at a children's matinee one year after its completion killing and crushing seventy-five youngsters — was none other than Farlow. He also knew Farlow had put rotten materials into the building of the cinema, and had bribed the inspector to pass them. The inspector in question was now serving a prison sentence. But Lance had spoken to him, and knew that although Farlow was able to prove he had no knowledge of the materials that had been used on the project, he had personally arranged for the job to be done cheaply.

Then there was the Norkington Town Hall tragedy: another of Farlow's affairs, reputedly fireproof, but which had gone up in flames, trapping thirty-two councilors and five employees in its raging interior. There had been other similar happenings; there was little Sebastian Farlow wouldn't poke his greedy fingers in, if he thought he would profit thereby. He was one of what Lance classified in his mind as the 'ungentlemanly.'

And 'the Knight's' method of dealing with the 'ungentlemanly' was rather ungentlemanly itself. Which was exactly why he had built up such a reputation for himself; and why police and crooks hated him and his interference, and the average man thanked God for men like him. For certain men whose methods were crooked, but within the law, owed certain extremely unpleasant happenings entirely to the Knight. He was a name, a legend, to be feared and watched by all those without a conscience. They knew that, the lawless element; they knew they might keep within the law of England, and yet transgress the Knight's laws, for he made his own. He was policeman, judge and jury — and often executioner.

The Knight watched, apparently uninterested, as Farlow talked rapidly to the dark lady. She seemed troubled, and in fact he thought there were tears bright in her deep, mysteriously intoxicating eyes. Tears that might at any given moment be shed.

Farlow talked on, and the Knight had reason again to thank the gods of adventure who had inspired him to learn the art of lip-reading. With its aid, he could tell almost every word Farlow said.

'You'll do it,' Farlow was saying almost viciously, the words leaving the side of his mouth, and his eyes scowling at the lady. 'If you don't, by God, you'll be sorry! And you'll do it within the next three weeks!'

She was shaking her head, half-dazedly, as if unable to grasp the enormity of the thing he asked.

Farlow snapped on: 'Remember that there's your family to think of. You know our power; you know what we can do. It isn't just your own life.'

Her lips moved, almost whispering: 'I — I can't. Don't — please don't ask me

. . . I — I couldn't do it.'

'I'm not asking you. I'm telling you. It's for the sake of your own country — your own people.'

'No — no!' she said vehemently. 'It isn't. I know it isn't. It's for you. You and the rest of them, so you can — can make more and more of your filthy money.'

Farlow looked at her darkly; then he turned and beckoned to a man who had been standing at the exit door. He was tall and broad, dressed in a long dark coat; his features were concealed by the brim of a large Homburg hat. But as he approached the table, he swept this off and bowed to the lady.

She started back with a gasp of terror. Her eyes rested wildly on the cold high-cheekboned face she saw; the coal-black glittering eyes like those of a venomous snake; the thin bloodless lips that suggested screams in the night and untold cruelty.

The Knight's interest quickened as he watched the second man speaking; the fellow was talking in some foreign language he did not understand, but his words seemed to be having a terrible effect upon the woman. Her eyes almost started out of her head; her hands were clenched on the tablecloth. She sat stiff and white, hardly seeming to breathe.

Then the man had finished speaking, and was looking at her with an unspoken question in his unblinking eyes, and — she nodded. Just a slight inclination of the head, but it spelled assent. And the Knight knew they had won; that whatever the second man had said had forced down all her resistance to their suggestions.

The second man bowed low again, replaced his hat, clicked his heels in military fashion, and walked straight across the floor and through the exit. Farlow rose and said: 'I thought Carlos would make you see reason. And now we have finally found out where you have been hiding from us. I must caution you not to try and dodge again, otherwise we shall have little mercy on your family. Good night . . . ' He paused, then added sneeringly: ' . . . your majesty!'

Adventure was eternally rearing its

fascinating head for Lance Knight, and he was ever ready to welcome it with open arms. Here was adventure of the highest order — the ingredients of a first-rate story had been attractively spread out for him. 'Your majesty' — that alone would have intrigued him. Then there was the thin white-faced man, so much like a walking corpse — Farlow, the crooked financier; and the darkly veiled threat to the woman's family.

It was the first scene of the first act; and though the other diners were unaware of it, the Knight could already hear the bugles of adventure and high endeavour fanfaring in his consciousness, with a clarion call he could no more have resisted than he could have turned his back on: some unfortunate who needed help.

A damsel in distress!

And the Knight — whose heart and mind would have stood out gloriously at the court of King Arthur centuries ago — rose from his table, and moved gallantly towards the lady.

She was dabbing at her liquid eyes with

an equally liquid scrap of handkerchief; and he didn't miss seeing the tiny crest and monogram upon that handkerchief, even though he could not place it. Then she had seen him above her, and crumpled the scrap of chiffon in her hand, and had banished the worry from her face. She looked at him questioningly. 'Yes? You're not a waiter, are you?'

There was the least trace of a foreign inflection in her voice. He smiled. 'I suppose you guessed that by the fact that my dress clothes don't fit me. No, I'm not a waiter. My name's Knight — Lance Knight.'

'It sounds very chivalrous, Mr. Knight. What can I do for you?'

He smiled at her encouragingly and sat down. 'Nothing. I've come along to do something for you, Miss . . . ?'

Her eyes opened in a stare. 'For me?'

'Just that. Now suppose we order wine, and make merry? I can recommend the cellars here — they keep only the best.'

She shook her head. 'I'm sorry, Mr. Knight, but I really don't care for wine just at the moment. Nor do I care to spend my time talking to strange young men whom I do not know.'

'But you do know me,' he insisted. 'I've already introduced myself, with all possible courtesy. It's your turn, isn't it?'

'I haven't the least intention of introducing myself.'

'You haven't?' He slid out his cigarette case. 'Mind if I smoke?' He lit one and repeated: 'You haven't? Then suppose I just call you . . . your majesty?'

Her handkerchief fell from her fingers onto the table. He reached for it, but she picked it up before him and thrust it into her pocket. Her eyes were wild and strained again. She gasped: 'I — I don't understand you. What — what do you mean?'

'It isn't very surprising,' he countered. 'I don't know your real name, but you most certainly look as if you might be a queen, or at least a princess.'

Her relief was obvious. She strove to smile, and laughed gently. 'You're very flattering, Mr. Knight, but surely you don't actually expect to find queens wandering about London unescorted?'

'Why not?' he asked her impudently. 'You find businessmen and garbage collectors. Why not queens?'

'Why — I — I don't really know. I thought — aren't they rather above that sort of thing?'

'Are they? No, I don't think so. Then you aren't a queen?'

She shook her head, smiling.

'Not even a princess?'

'Not that, even.'

'Then you must be a duchess, is that it?'

'No. I'm just an ordinary woman, Mr. Knight. I don't see why you should be so anxious to give me a throne. I assure you I would have no idea of the first thing to do if I were a queen, but I most certainly wouldn't be wandering through London alone. My name, if it will set your mind at ease, is Janis Smith.'

'Smith?' said the Knight reflectively. 'Now where have I heard that name before? Unusual, isn't it?'

'You don't believe me?'

'Afraid not. I have an idea you're in trouble of some kind, and I'd like to help.

Those men you were talking to — '

A trace of fear crept into her eyes. 'You — you heard?'

He shook his head. She wouldn't have much confidence in him if she thought he'd eavesdropped on a private conversation. 'I heard nothing. But Farlow, the fat man, is a noted bad hat. He's so bad he's positively rotten. Whenever he stays at a hotel, they disinfect his room after him. Pigs have been known to refuse to eat with him anywhere near their sties.'

'I know,' she said. 'But you needn't worry. He's only a casual acquaintance.'

'And the other chappie. The Zombie — how about him?'

'I hardly know him. He happens to be a friend of Farlow's. He wished to be introduced to me, and Farlow obliged. That was all. So you see, there isn't any need for your help after all.'

The Knight considered. Then he said earnestly: 'Please believe that I'm sincere in my desire to help you, Miss — er — *Smith*. I have every reason to believe you're in great trouble, and trouble's my hobby. The women I've helped in the past, if — assuming it were possible — they were placed end to end in a line, would reach from here to Wapping.'

'But I don't want to be part of that line, Mr. Knight. I'd object very strongly. And I'm rather tired of the subject now. If you wish to buy me some wine, please do so, but don't let's talk. I'm not in trouble of any kind.'

The Knight shrugged. She eyed him keenly and said worriedly: 'Are you sure you didn't overhear our conversation?'

'Not a syllable.'

'Then — then why are you so determined to think I'm in trouble of some kind? Why did you call me — your majesty?'

'Why not? You look the kind of woman who might be in a jam; and in any case, I wanted to meet you. You're quite the most beautiful thing that's ever happened to this restaurant. You aren't an English-woman, are you?'

'I am,' she said with too much assertion to carry conviction.

'But — the foreign accent?'

'I've spent a little time abroad, and I

had a foreign nursemaid when I was young,' she replied evasively.

He shook his head. 'I still think you're being deliberately misleading, Janis,' he said, and the smile he gave her took the sting out of the impertinence of his words. 'You don't look in character here as an ordinary woman. Your bearing's different.'

'Really? In what way?'

'I'll put an adjective to it. 'Regal' is the word.'

Her eyes narrowed. 'Why must you insist on making royalty of me?'

'I don't know. It may have been the way your late companion — the sheet-faced gentleman — bowed to you, and the way you accepted that bow, as if it were something you were accustomed to; something that was your right.'

She stood up, irritated. 'You're boring me. Please go away.'

'Not yet. I haven't finished talking.'

'You have — quite finished. Good night, Mr. Knight.'

He stood up as she began to move away. 'I'll come along.'

She turned, regarding him coldly. 'If you do, I shall call the first policeman I meet and have you given in charge.'

Then she was gone towards the ladies' cloakroom, and he sighed and made for the gentlemen's cloakroom. He checked out his hat and coat, put them on, and stood outside the entrance to the place in a cluster of shadows thrown by the ornamental gargoyles above the entrance.

Janis came out ten minutes later; her face was quite pale, and she was twisting her handbag with gloved fingers nervously. She peered each way along the street, and failing to spot him in the shadows, started walking rapidly along.

The Strand was crowded, and he found it easy to keep pace almost directly behind her. Not once did she glance round, for her mind seemed set on some clear destination. As they turned the corner, a red bus roared towards them — and dropping her handbag on the pavement, the mysterious woman threw herself directly in its path, to an accompaniment of hoarse cries and screeching brakes . . .

2

In Which a Knight Comes to the Rescue

The whole thing happened so unexpectedly, so spontaneously, that only the Knight, who had been on the woman's heels, knew just what was really going on.

Suicide!

The bus driver was taken by surprise; and although he applied his brakes at once, and hard, Janis would have stood no chance but for Lance Knight. Almost before she had begun to fall, with the bus a mere screaming ten feet away from her, he was by her side and had thrown his arm about her waist. Then, without a pause, he dragged her to the safety of the other pavement.

A car tearing from behind the bus screeched in protest, swerved to avoid them, and piled itself up against a lamp standard; the traffic behind the bus piled hopelessly into the rear of the bus, and confusion reigned. People were still screaming, their senses not yet attuned to the fact that the woman had been dragged from death at the crucial moment. The bus driver was white and shaky, hands hot and trembling on the brake handle.

A portentous policeman pushed his way towards the road, looking about for the woman and her rescuer. ''Ello,' he said, puzzled. 'Where the 'ell are they?'

'She did it purposely,' shrieked a woman behind him. 'I saw her. Tried to commit suicide, she did. I saw her.'

'We knows, we knows,' agreed the constable. 'An' we'll likely 'ave to see into it. But wot I wants to know is, where the 'ell 'ave they got to?'

He endeavoured to peer across the road where a crowd surged about the wrecked car that had hit the lamp standard. He strode imperiously across to seek the missing would-be suicide and her deliverer. He searched, like Moses of old, and found not — they had flown.

While all the bustle and excitement raged, not ten yards away, in a public house saloon lounge, the Knight was ordering brandy and eyeing the shaking Janis curiously.

He hadn't paused at the scene of the rescue. He knew she had tried to kill herself; knew there were plenty of people to verify that fact. And he also knew the English law. It was almost as grave an offence to take your own life as to take the life of someone else. Had Janis remained, there would have been awkward questions; and had she been unable to answer them satisfactorily, there would have been trouble.

He had hustled right onto the pavement, and while attention had concentrated itself on the crashing car, had steered her rapidly into the pub. Now she was dithering frightfully, but she didn't look at all like a young lady who had been salvaged from death. She was lost between a violent attack of nerves and a bout of accusation of her rescuer.

She said slowly but angrily: 'You again! Why must you interfere? Why, when I had screwed my nerve up to the sticking point? Oh, God, why didn't you leave me alone, you fool?'

The Knight's tone was no longer bantering. He said: 'I don't approve of suicide. It's the fool's way out.'

'You don't understand. If you hadn't stopped me, it would all have been over now.'

'Would it? Suppose you had only been dreadfully injured? Suppose you had lain for weeks, months, years in some hospital in terrible agony? Would it have been over?'

Suddenly she broke into a spasm of sobbing, and he drew the tiny curtain across their booth and patted her shoulder. 'The bus wasn't going fast enough to have killed you, but it might have seriously damaged you for life.'

She shuddered. 'I see that, now you've told me.'

'And the driver — how would he have felt? Did you think of that? Could you put yourself in his place? He might have lost his nerve and never driven again. Lost his livelihood.'

'I — I'm sorry.' It was a whisper from

beneath the handkerchief with which she was dabbing at her cheeks. It was a contrite whisper; her exploit had knocked the props of her self-assurance away, and she hung her head, ashamed.

The Knight smiled. 'I'm going to be frank with you. There're more ways of committing suicide than one. Tell me your story, and if I can't put things right in some measure for you, I'll personally hand you some tablets that you can take and never wake again from. Fair?'

She shook her head. 'No — I don't want to commit suicide as such. I want it to look like an accidental death. I — I want them to think so. That's why I tried the method I did, so that they'd read about it in the paper and think it was an accident.'

'Who are 'they'?'

'Farlow and Carlos, and the others. All of them. You see, if I was killed, I wouldn't be able to do as they ask. And if I was killed accidentally, they could hardly blame me, could they? And if they couldn't blame me, they couldn't very well torture mother and father, and

— and my sister and brother.'

The Knight controlled his curiosity with admirable patience. He didn't force her to talk; he waited until the brandy arrived and gave the barman a pound note for the doubles, telling him to keep the change. He watched Janis sip hers at his request, smiling when she coughed and spluttered. A hint of colour returned to her cheeks.

'Won't you trust me, even now?' he said.

'I can't do that. Besides, it's my own affair, and I'd hate to drag anyone else into it. They'd stoop to anything to get what they want, even murder.'

'The more you say, the more I feel I must know what the trouble's about. I've already told you that if you'll tell me the whole trouble, and I can't help, I'll fix it so that you can commit suicide that will look like an accident. I'm pretty sure I can give you a hand, otherwise I wouldn't be saying that. And the alternative, if you choose not to tell me, is the police.'

'Police?' she stammered.

'That's right. The bobbies here have

some quaint laws, one of which says no one must take a life, not even their own.'

'You'd — you'd turn me over to them?'

He nodded. 'I would, but only for your own sake. Just to prevent you trying again.' His eyes fastened upon the handkerchief she held, which in her agitation was fully exposed. He saw the crest again, and remembered. 'You're Princess Janis of Lazania. Isn't that right?'

She seemed about to deny it, but then her shoulders slumped and she nodded hopelessly.

'When civil war broke out in your country, you were in England. Before you had time to even start on your journey home, the rebels had overthrown the throne, seized power, and held your father the king, your mother the queen, and your sister and brother in captivity in the castle at Lazan, the capital city.'

Again she nodded, then faced him bravely. 'I will trust you, Mr. Knight. The rebels — who call themselves the Korvinites, and are led by their dictator, Gustave Korvin, a beast of a man — had, as you say, seized power before I could return. All the other great powers have decided on a policy of non-intervention, for our country is really absurdly small, and its population is not so great as that of greater London. I had no option but to remain in London myself; and there news of my country's change of rule and the imprisonment of my family was brought to me by my cousin, Count Eric Dornich, who had managed to escape one jump ahead of the army of Korvinites. And he brought with him the plans — '

'Plans?'

'Yes; the entire rebellion was inspired by those plans — they caused the revolution. You see, for a long time, Father had thought there was oil in our country's territory. Finally he had experts drilling, sounding, and there was oil! Korvin, who was at that time a minister of state, and in Father's confidence, had a powerful following among the peasants, and the bandits who lurk in the hills robbing coaches and motorcars that pass through our land. There is no railway line across it, for the country has never been rich enough to install one, and no one else has thought it worth the trouble of exploiting. But these new oil concessions meant wealth to us, and we were approached by several businessmen who wished to secure them. Father didn't wish to dispose of them at all. They were to be worked by our own people, and any profit was to go to the common good. That was when Korvin stepped in and tried to persuade Father to utilise the find for the good of the upper classes. Father refused, and Korvin left the castle, took headquarters, and rallied all his supporters to his banner.

'He attacked while Father was totally unprepared; and half the Lazanian army laid down arms without oven fighting, for we only maintained them for ceremonial purposes. Korvin had won, but my cousin Count Dornich escaped with the plans — the only plans in existence of the location of the oil fields!

'If you know Lazania, you'd realise just how hopeless it would be to find those particular spots again without plans. It was really only luck that made the experts hit on them in the first place; and it is

27

common knowledge that Korvin secured financial help in his revolution from someone who badly wanted the concessions, and to whom he intended to grant a monopoly the moment he was in power. Now they are probably pressing him, and he doesn't know where the fields are.'

'But surely he could get in touch with the experts who first found them?'

'That would hardly help him, for they could never find their way to them again without a map. And the map was drawn up by Eric, my cousin, so that only he knows the exact location.'

'And where do you come into this?'

'They know quite well Eric will never reveal the secret, no matter what threats they make. He intends to use the promise of concessions to persuade the countries who want oil to step in and take power from Korvin. Only I know where he is staying, and where he is negotiating from. Only I know where the plans are hidden. Only I can get it. And today Farlow, who is working on behalf of Korvin, found out I was staying at the home of Father's friend, Colonel Mercer. He sent me a note containing references to my captured relatives, and hinting disastrous things would happen to them unless I obeyed his orders — the first of which was to meet him for lunch or dinner at Sylvester's Restaurant. I met him for dinner, and . . . he threatened again that if I didn't secure the plans, my family would suffer. This time I — I agreed.'

'And who was the man with him?'

'Baron Carlos Blud. He's horrible.' She shuddered. 'He's a sadistic fanatic, who truly believes in everything Korvin says or does. He thinks Korvin is working for the good of Lazania. He is chief of Korvin's army, and Korvin's second in command. He's over here solely for the purpose of telling me what will happen to my parents if I don't cooperate. I think I'm more frightened of Blud than any of the others.'

'I don't blame you,' agreed the Knight. 'He does look as if he would be capable of roaring with laughter every time he saw anyone jabbed with a sword. And Farlow — whereabouts does he come into it all?'

'I'm not too sure.'

'Is he the man who wants the oil concessions?'

She shook her head. 'I think not. But I believe he's working in that man's interests. I know Eric told me he got in touch with Korvin first, so it must be that.'

The Knight nodded and looked at her compassionately. 'And you thought if you could make them think you'd died in an accident, they wouldn't be able to use you as a tool for their game? You thought they couldn't very well take it out on your family, if you weren't alive to know it.'

'Yes; they've given me a few weeks to get the plans. But I don't know what to do. I'd hate to play a trick like that on poor Eric. He risked his life to get the plans away, and he hopes that with them he can persuade other powers to take action against Korvin.'

'He may be able to do so, but it'll be a long and tedious job. And meanwhile, your parents are imprisoned and at the mercy of Korvin and his merry men. Well, we'll see what we can root out of the tangle. I said I'd help, and by heaven I will. If I can get my fingers round the throat of the man who's caused all this simply to grab off a few oil wells, I'll wring his bloated neck! If anyone can give orders that your family are not to be harmed, he's the man. And if I can't get him before two weeks are out, damn it, I'll fly to Lazania myself and fight the entire blasted army!'

And when she looked at the reckless, laughing, devil-may-care eyes in his lean tanned features; when she saw the set of his strong, square jaw and suppleness of his muscles under his immaculate dress suit, she knew he'd be capable of doing even that.

And the Knight himself had no doubts — it was high time he indulged in another crusade!

* * *

Sebastian Farlow was saying: 'I think we've fixed it all up, sir. The woman's under our thumb. Three weeks I've given her, and if she doesn't produce the plans by then, we'll have to persuade her by forwarding one of her sister's fingers to her.'

The deep voice at the other end of the phone said: 'Make it as quick as possible, Farlow. We don't want that fool Count Dornich to hold those plans any longer than we can help. As long as he has them, there's a chance of his persuading some other country to step in.'

'Meanwhile, couldn't Korvin put men to search for the location of the experimental wells?'

'He has done, but they can't find any trace of the ones that contain oil. God alone knows where they are.'

'Suppose we get hold of the men who prospected for them?'

'I've thought of that. There were two of them, but both are now in America. And they're both friends of the king's. They wouldn't talk even if we could get them over to Lazania.'

'Then I'll do all I can, sir.'

'It will be to your advantage, Farlow. Remember, a tenth share in those wells isn't to be sneezed at.'

Farlow hung the telephone back on its

rest, lit a cigar, and sat back at his desk at his ease. This promised to be very profitable, if everything worked out all right — and he didn't see what could go wrong, now that Princess Janis was terrified enough to get the plan for them.

He sighed, looked out of the long slightly open French windows at the dark lawn — and saw a moving shadow that was out of place in that quietude. He started, then stepped from his desk towards the window. He knew that Baron Blud, Korvin's emissary, was given to prowling in the dark for no obvious reason. Farlow was actually afraid of Blud; but since the man's help was needed, he had been forced to extend a room at his own home to the sadistic Korvinite. He peered into the dark garden and called: 'Baron — that you?'

Now there was no sound except the screeching of two cats close at hand. The long lawn and the high wall beyond were as they had always been. There was no suggestion of anyone prowling there.

Farlow laughed nervously at his own imagination, walked back to his desk, sat behind it, and began to write a letter. Suddenly his eyes shifted to the window again. He tensed. Again he called, and again he received no answer.

He continued with the letter, but now his eyes darted furtive glances towards the blackness outside involuntarily. He had a strange feeling of being watched, spied upon.

And then the shadow came again, and this time it stayed!

It not only stayed, but it actually advanced upon the window and walked through into the room. Farlow faced someone he did not know; someone who wore dark clothing and no hat, and whose lean laughing face looked at him mockingly as he shuddered back in his chair.

The stranger said: 'Good evening, Mr. Farlow — or may I call you Sebastian? My name is Knight.'

3

In Which Mr. Farlow is Disturbed

Farlow sat frozen at his desk, mouth open. His hand was actually halfway towards the bell-push to summon help in case the dark man should be a hold-up merchant, but at these words all life seemed to leave Farlow's gross frame. He sat as petrified as if he had been suddenly turned to stone.

At length his lips moved slowly. Hoarsely he said: 'Knight? The man they call — the — 'the Knight'?'

Lance, waiting patiently for him to recover his wits, nodded with considerable pleasure. 'I'm glad to see you've heard of me, Farlow. You'll know just what and who I am, won't you?'

Farlow made a great effort, allowing the hand that had been streaking for the bell-push to continue its journey. And like a flash of lightning, the Knight's hand travelled to his side pocket and emerged holding an automatic.

He pointed it airily at Farlow and rapped: 'I wouldn't. I'd hate to have to knock your fifth waistcoat button off before we've even exchanged views about the weather. No, don't reach for that bell, Farlow — and don't try any funny tricks of any other description.'

Farlow wheezed: 'You're — you're bluffing! You — you wouldn't shoot!'

The Knight smiled. 'Perhaps I wouldn't, Sebastian. But if you really want to find out, go ahead and ring that bell.'

Farlow didn't want to find out that badly. He relaxed and grated: 'What do you want here? I know your record, and I warn you that if you interfere in any way with me, I'll see the police do something about you.'

The Knight appropriated one of Farlow's cigars, then smelt and lit it single-handed. The blue-black muzzle of his gun didn't waver from its bead on the financier's midriff. He blew out smoke thoughtfully, looked hard at Farlow, then smiled. 'I don't expect it's going to be too easy to find out anything from you, Sebby,' he said genially. 'But if you won't talk of your own free will, perhaps I can make you . . . what do you think?'

Farlow half rose in fear and whined: 'If you touch me, Knight . . . '

'Oh, I shan't touch you, my fat friend. I wouldn't do that, not even with a fifteen-foot barge pole. I value my health far too much; and to me, Sebby, you look as if you might be contagious. But I wouldn't need to touch you, would I? I mean I could walk you out of here, into my car, and drive you down to a little place I have near Land's End. There's a cliff just there, and if you happened to fall over it on to the jagged rocks beneath, I'm afraid your insurance company would be paying out on . . . accidental death.'

'You — you wouldn't. You're bluffing,' whispered Farlow; but under the bantering tone he knew the Knight was tense, cold steel. He could tell that by his eyes — as hard and bright as diamonds, with chips of steel shifting in the grey pupils.

'So perhaps,' went on the Knight,

'you'd like to talk to me now, Sebby. Do tell me all about it.'

Farlow reached nervously for one of his cigars, clipped off the end and inserted it in his lips. He lit and drew on it, holding it in shaking fingers. 'What do you want with me, Knight? I'm a straightforward, honest businessman — I can't be of any interest to your kind. You only bother crooks, or so the newspapers say.'

'Dear Sebby,' drawled the Knight mockingly, 'so naïve! So innocent. If I didn't know better, I'd think you'd never heard of a certain cinema that collapsed on a crowded audience of kids, or of a well-known 'fireproof' civic centre that burnt down. But unfortunately for you, I do know of them, and of many more besides. So don't try to pull any wool over my eyes, Sebastian. I know quite well you're bad to the the bottom. No — don't deny it.'

'I wasn't going to,' said Farlow. 'Those were legitimate business deals. I had no way of knowing the place would collapse.'

'Didn't you? You put rotten materials in the construction and you took care to efface yourself from any responsibility. Now if you thought it wasn't going to collapse, why go to that trouble? Tell me that.'

Farlow growled: 'You can't prove anything. All that's over and forgotten. Not even you could make the police believe I had anything to do with it!'

The Knight crossed his legs, sitting nonchalantly on one edge of Farlow's desk. 'No, I couldn't prove anything. But I don't need to, Sebby. I act as my own judge and jury, and my own executioner. You should know that by now. It's all true, you see. The police can't pin anything on to me, and I don't think a jury would do more than convict me on a manslaughter charge if they did. I only kill rats. And you, Sebby, look exactly like a rat to me — a large, fat bloated rat!'

Farlow didn't speak; his eyes were fixed on that gun, and terror was dawning in his face. He recalled some of the stories he had heard and read about the Knight, and his blood ran cold. There was good reason for half the crooks in England to go in fear of Lance Knight — very good reason.

The Knight heaved a sigh. 'But I haven't come here to bandy chit-chat with you. Nor have I trotted along to argue about what you've done in the past. It's what you're doing right now that interests me.'

'I don't understand you.'

'You will, brother, you will. I have no fear of that, Sebby. I'll make myself perfectly plain. I wish to know who is employing you as a stooge in connection with the Lazanian oil plans.'

Farlow couldn't have jumped higher if he'd sat on a pin. His great bulk rose at least three inches from his chair, his eyes stalked from his head, and his mouth gave an impersonation of an open manhole. The Knight regarded him sadly.

'I've given you a shock? Dear me, I'm sorry. But you look as if you're about to deny any knowledge of the whole thing. If you are, don't! If there's one thing I dislike more than a crook who doesn't tell the truth, I don't know what it is. Just tell me who told you to get in touch with

Princess Janis of Lazania about the plans, and then I'll let you toddle off to bed like a good boy.'

'I don't know — ' began Farlow.

' — what I'm talking about,' concluded the Knight. 'I didn't think you would. And that's going to make everything very awkward — for you.'

It happened before Farlow could even yelp. Like a steel sprung spring, the Knight uncoiled his long limbs from his perch and moved. Farlow didn't even see him clearly in the next few seconds — he knew only that there was a blur at the side of his desk, and then the impact of a set of granite-like knuckles lifted him backwards over his chair and threw him sickeningly to the floor. He lay quite prostrate, blood trickling from one side of his mouth.

The Knight rubbed his knuckles reflectively and murmured: 'The dear boy. I'm afraid I've hurt him a little. Too bad. But he really should brush up on his hospitality a bit. He wasn't very chummy at all.'

He stooped and got his hands beneath

the unconscious Farlow's shoulders. Then, as if Farlow had been no more than a child, he lifted him easily into the chair behind the desk over which he had catapulted, and sat down on the desk to wait events.

Farlow came round in about five minutes, with much mumbling and some spitting of blood. He opened his eyes, saw the Knight, and opened his mouth to yell.

The Knight displayed a rock-like fist warningly, and brandished it a few inches before Farlow's nose. Farlow cut the yell before it left his lips. He was snow-white, his eyes panicky, his breath coming hard, his entire body cringing before the anticipated blow.

'And now that you've seen how easily you bruise,' drawled the Knight laconically, 'perhaps you'll remember a few things you didn't seem to know about before you tasted my knuckles. Or do you want a second helping?'

Farlow rubbed his aching jaws gingerly and whimpered: 'Look here, Knight. I'm not denying anything — it isn't worthwhile. But I'm telling you, you can't prove anything, whatever you know. And you can't know very much, or you wouldn't need to come here to me for additional information.'

The Knight smiled charmingly and studied his fingers. 'Perhaps you'd like me to take off this diamond ring before I hit you again, Sebastian? It may cut, you know.'

Farlow winced and drew back in his chair. He snarled: 'If you lay another finger on me, Knight, I'll sue you for everything you've got, and chance what you'll try and pin on me. Isn't there any easier way out than this? Surely you aren't in this for anything but money for nothing. Well, if that's all you want, you can have it. Five thousand pounds here and now to lay off me and the oil plan!'

And the Knight didn't even blink. 'Done! Where's the money?'

Farlow wheezed: 'Hold on a minute. How do I know I can trust you to lay off after you get it?'

'You don't,' explained the Knight sweetly. 'That's your hard luck. But one thing's certain — if you don't hand it over, I'll refuse any further offers like it, and go on and smash you. You also know I mean that, and that I'm quite capable of it.'

Farlow nodded, crossed to a safe in the wall, and twiddled the combination. He talked while he did so, saying: 'How did you get on to all this? I suppose Princess Janis came to you for help?'

'She did not,' said Knight calmly. 'I lip-read your conversation in the restaurant tonight. And here's another warning for you: if Janis gets hurt, you'll get hurt — badly. You understand that?'

Farlow understood it all right; he could hardly return to the desk because of the way his knees were shaking. He laid a pile of neatly stacked notes before the Knight, and Lance counted them rapidly.

'Good. Just five thousand.' He smiled. 'Now if you'll give me a statement.'

'Statement?' whined Farlow. 'How d'you mean?'

The Knight studied him pityingly. 'Really, Sebby, you must think I was born yesterday. I'm not that dumb, you know. I have no doubt that once I've sped away with this little haul, you'll call the police and inform them I've held you up and robbed you. And I very much dislike police stations and policemen. They ask so many unnecessary questions. So if you'll sign a little note of hand, saying you paid me five thousand pounds for services rendered, I'll feel much easier about the whole thing, won't I? Start writing, Sebastian!'

Farlow grunted, reached for a pen, and started to draft out the required note. The Knight took and read it, nodded, and folded it with the money which he stuffed carelessly in his pocket. Then he grinned. 'This is damned generous of you, Sebastian. How does it feel to be a public benefactor?'

Farlow started and looked narrowly at him. 'I don't know what you mean.'

'Of course not. You think you've paid me this to drop my interest in you, don't you? You should know better than that, laddie. As far as I'm concerned, this money is merely a donation to the children's hospitals. You'll know how hard-pressed for money they are, won't you, Sebby? And you'll know how hard they work — particularly how hard they worked that day when your rotten building collapsed, and sent them more patients than they could handle. Still, five thousand will help to make amends in some measure, and I bet they'll be quite surprised when they receive so much from an anonymous donor. Won't you feel proud to read about it in the papers?'

Farlow stammered: 'Then — then you were just lying? You've no intention of leaving me alone?'

'Less now than ever,' the Knight told him, grinning. 'I see that first punch of mine improved the appearance of your features — perhaps a second will improve them even more so. Your nose is a bit askew, isn't it? Hold still and I'll try to put it straight for you.'

From somewhere Farlow suddenly found a supply of courage; he was seated at his desk again, and he reached casually for the drawer from which he had taken the paper to write the note — then his hand became a darting streak, and his fingers curled about the gun that lay there . . .

It was an unfortunate move from his point of view; for although the Knight had put away his gun, he was not caught napping. His hand, which had been resting on a heavy metal pen rack, swept upwards and downwards. Farlow's semi-bald head was subjected to a blow like the kick of a donkey; and for the second time that night he made overtures to the hard floor.

He seemed to be out for a long time this time; Lance settled him comfortably, examined the wound on his head, and saw it was not very serious. Then he search rapidly through the man's desk, finding little of interest.

The safe beckoned him invitingly; his eyes had watched Farlow at work on it, and noted the combinations. There was little the Knight's eyes missed — he owed his life many times over to his quickness and perception.

The safe swung open within seconds; he thumbed through the contents speedily, glancing cursorily at the documents and papers therein. There was nothing relating to the Lazanian oil wells. He glanced regretfully at the money still inside; but he was careful not to touch any of it, for he knew Farlow would have welcomed the opportunity to put the police on his track.

Finally he swung the safe door shut, then looked at Farlow again. He was still out, and showed no sign of recovery.

The Knight stood there, thinking out his next move. It was certain he couldn't wait around until Farlow recovered, and it was also certain he would learn nothing. He doubted if any amount of beating up would drag the truth from the financier. There were some things Farlow valued above his own miserable carcass, and the money that could be made from an oil field was doubtless one of them.

The Knight sighed. He had hoped for better luck than this. He turned reluctantly towards the window . . .

And the phone rang!

He slithered round the desk, scooped the receiver up, and said 'Sebastian Farlow speaking' in a passable imitation of the other man's voice. The voice that replied was not very clear; and it was gruff and masculine, which added to the vagueness of it. But the words it spoke made the Knight tighten his grip on the phone until the knuckles of his hand stood out white against the ebonite.

'Farlow? Good, I hoped I'd catch you in your study. Listen — I've found out where Count Dornich is staying. I've sent two men to attend to him — you know what I mean? We should have the plans by tomorrow morning, if he keeps it on him. You know I don't want to appear personally in this thing, so you'll collect the plans from these men. You know them. They're the two cut-throats you told me to hire if I needed any rough business doing. I connected with them by phone, told them I was you, and gave them their orders. If they get the plans, they'll bring them to your home first thing in the morning, and you are to pay them five hundred pounds each. Got all that?'

'Yes,' husked Lance, keeping tight hold of his nerve. 'Where is Dornich staying?'

'Somewhere we'd never have expected to find him — at the home of the Lazanian foreign minister, the man who represented Lazania in England before the revolution. I also found out that the minister is due to attend a ball at the American Embassy tonight. And he's taking his wife with him, leaving only an old housekeeper and Dornich at home. It should be easy.'

Lance said: 'Listen — can I see you? There's a thing or two I'd like to get straight.'

'You know damn well you can't see me,' snapped the other, and the phone clicked annoyingly as he hung up.

The Knight said: 'Operator — I'm a police detective. Will you trace that call I just took?'

He waited, fuming with impatience. It was a long wait. During it, Farlow started to stir, and groaned feebly. Lance tapped him thoughtfully on the head again with the pen rack, and he subsided.

'The call came from a public booth, sir,' intoned the operator, and Lance thanked her and hung up. He was sure he had been in touch with the organising brain behind all this trouble. But he was no nearer finding out in whose head that brain reposed. When he did, that head was destined to be very sore.

Meanwhile, Count Dornich was in immediate danger. And Lance had no time to lose. He crossed the room to the door in long strides and grabbed the handle. Then he paused, chilled by an eerie presentiment of danger — danger behind that door. As he stood there the door opened, and the white, grotesque face of Baron Carlos Blud stared in!

4

In Which a Murder is Committed

Blud's fish-like eyes took in the scene in one breathless moment; and then his gaze shifted to the Knight, without venom or malice, and he regarded him curiously.

'Step in, my friend,' said the Knight, for now the danger had materialised, he was once again cool and collected. He stood inside the door carelessly, but keyed for instant action.

Blud waved one pallid, clammy, corpse-like hand towards the slumbering Farlow. He said: 'You do — this?'

'I expect I must have done. Yes, I believe I did.'

'Why?'

The Knight scratched his head. 'It's rather a long story, you see. But to boil it all down, I just don't like Sebby's face — do you?'

Blud didn't smile; probably he didn't

understand, and if he had, he looked the kind of man who was devoid of any sense of humour. He gave the Knight a fishy stare, then his stare intensified as he noted the gun the Knight had produced.

'Gun?' he said enquiringly. 'Why?'

'The universal language, brother,' said the Knight tautly. 'I told you I didn't like Sebastian's face; I don't. But he was a positive beauty compared to you. I'd say, at a guess, you were a character from Bram Stoker's *Dracula*. That's the way you look. But skip that — and step carefully into the room, will you, laddie?' And he gestured with his gun.

Blud stood for one second on the threshold; then, seeming to acquiesce, he stepped forward and passed the Knight. At that point it was Lance's intention to reverse the automatic and bring it down upon the baron's totally bald skull. But something misfired — for once the Knight was up against a brain as keen as his own, and his plan flopped.

Blud might not speak the English language very well; but when it came to cunning in personal warfare he was all there, and punctual with it. His heavily booted leg scuffed out sideways, and as it smacked home against the Knight's shin, he half-revolved and sent his fist spinning after it, connecting with the Knight's jaw like a steam hammer.

The Knight was taken completely by surprise; his legs bent under the impact, and the gun slithered to the floor. He gained a hazy impression that he had somehow become entangled in a bout with Joe Louis. But he gripped hard on his reeling senses, and made an astonishing recovery.

His eyes focused clearly again upon the Baron, bending low to pick up the fallen automatic. The temptation was irresistible, and the Knight succumbed. His right foot travelled forward, beautifully timed and placed. The Baron gave one sharp harking yell and a lurid curse in his own language, then sprawled head forward into the room.

'And if that,' mused the Knight, darting outside, slamming the door and turning the key, 'doesn't make him hopping mad, I don't know what will!'

He wouldn't have objected to staying and continuing his attentions on Baron Blud. But there was no time — already two thugs might be on their way to see Count Dornich, and the Knight had an unaccountable yen to upset their apple cart.

The front door opened easily to his touch, and he was out in the dark streets. He had no idea of the name or address of the Lazanian ex-foreign minister, but he had infinite faith in the blue-clad minions of the London law. There was little those boys didn't know, in Lance's estimation; and accordingly he stopped the first constable he encountered.

'A sprightly evening, officer.'

'Not bad, sir,' agreed the constable, smiling patronisingly at him. 'Getting a bit chilly now, though.'

'Hmm. I hadn't noticed. By the way, they tell me you London bobbies are wonderful. Is this true?'

'I wouldn't know, sir,' replied the P.C. modestly. 'I don't count very much to myself, but I can't answer for the rest of us.'

'They tell me you know all kinds of outlandish facts,' went on the Knight. 'Such as, for instance, where the home of the Lazanian foreign minister is.'

The P.C. scratched his head. 'Well, now, I do happen to know that, sir. When the revolution was on over there, he asked for police protection — seems he was afraid of being assassinated or something. I happened to be one of his guards. He lives at number eighty-three, Gresham Terrace, Golders Green.'

'And you don't guard the chappie any longer?'

'Not now the revolution's over, sir.'

'I see. Well, Officer, I must agree with the person who gave you such high commendation. You are wonderful. I don't suppose more than one person in a hundred would know such a useful fact as that.'

'I don't know, sir. I think about three quarters of the force know that one.'

The Knight smiled at him admiringly. 'Have one with me, will you?'

Then he was gone, leaving the constable scratching his head and gazing blankly at the one-pound note in his hand.

The cab Lance took bore him rapidly towards Golders Green; he alighted intentionally about a hundred yards from Golders Green proper and went the rest of the way on the double. It was dark and silent down there; it was after one in the morning, and respectable people had long retired to the warm security of their beds. Only cats were abroad — cats and the Knight.

And he knew almost before he had reached Gresham Drive that he was too late; he knew that in his mind, and, like most of his hunches, he felt sure he was right.

He found eighty-three and went right in without a pause. If the dirty work was yet to be done, he would prevent it. If not, he would see what he could salvage from the adventure.

The house — a semi-Victorian affair — was in darkness. But the front door stood almost imperceptibly ajar. And form within came the sound of footsteps.

Two men appeared in the doorway as

he fell back in shadow. Two men who bore the stamp of the die-hard criminal. One was small and flashy, with a loud striped suit. The other was burly and dark and be-capped.

The flashy gentleman stepped out and peered all about him; and as he turned to whisper that the coast was clear, a hand shot from the shadows, and a gun butt played a triple tattoo on his soft felt hat. As he fell, the Knight stepped from the shadows, and the other thug stared foolishly into the muzzle of his gun.

'No monkey business,' warned the Knight. 'This little toy has a habit of going off when I press the trigger. And it doesn't squirt water.'

''Oo the 'ell — ?'

'Such language,' drawled the Knight. 'Really! Turn round, my foul-mouthed friend, whilst I frisk you for concealed weapons.'

The thug had no choice; he turned unwillingly, and once again the butt of the Knight's automatic sizzled down onto a skull — the cloth cap might as well not have been there for all the good it did. Its presence only made the Knight hit harder.

'How trusting these boys are,' sighed the Knight as the burly character made a duet of it with his flashy pal on the ground. 'I merely ask them to do something, and blow me if they don't do it. Comrade Farlow suffered from the same trustfulness — look how eagerly he made me a gift of five thousand. Ah, well.'

He stooped and went expertly through the pockets of the two slumbering cut-throats. He found what he was looking for on the person of the flashy man, and stood up with a triumphant smile. It was a long sealing-waxed envelope bearing the Lazanian coat of arms. The seal had been broken, and he slid out the contents, seeing the neatly drawn map. He slid the packet into his pocket and stepped delicately over the two thugs; then, on an afterthought, he turned back and treated them both to a further tap on the skulls.

The old housekeeper, a woman of about seventy, was lying inside the doorway, completely unconscious; on her temple a large blue bruise had sprung into being. He picked his way past her, along a short passage, and looked in at an open door on the left. That room was empty, and he wasted no time on it. He tried the next along, a study-cum-library. For a moment he thought he had struck unlucky here too; then he saw the nattily garbed feet protruding from the back of the desk, and knew his search was at an end.

Here was Count Dornich, lying motionless in a pool of his own blood, his head horribly smashed in, probably by the blood-stained iron bar that lay nearby. The Knight had seen death many times and often enough laughed in the face of it. But here was a man to whom death had come suddenly and gruesomely. From his position, it was evident he had been seated at his desk, back to the door. The thugs must have sneaked in and struck before he had been aware that he was not alone. It was mainly the back of the head which had suffered.

The Knight stood there for long seconds; seconds that ticked out from a clock on the desk; seconds in which he swore to himself to find the man behind the murder.

Then he went back to the step and picked up the unconscious men. He found rope round the side of the house, tied them both firmly together, and said: 'I'll leave these beauties for the police.'

The flashy gentleman stirred and, moaned, and the Knight watched him patiently. Finally he had recovered enough to be aware what had happened to him, and his greasy skin glistened with moisture as he eyed the Knight.

'Enjoy your little snooze?' asked the Knight conversationally and brightly. 'I hope so, because I'm afraid you aren't going to snooze again for some time. You'll be so worried at the idea of the hangman slipping that noose round your neck that you'll never be able to grab a wink.'

The flashy one panted with fear and desperation, eying the Knight pleadingly. 'Don't turn me in, mister. I don't know nothing about what happened back there. We — we found him like that, honest.'

The Knight shook his head. 'Sorry, but that won't do. I intend to park you both back in the house and telephone for the police. I won't stay to meet them, but I've no doubt the housekeeper will be able to tell them as much as they need know when she comes round. And if I were you, I'd advise you to tell the police just who put you up to this murder.'

'I will,' coughed the little man viciously. 'By God I will. He said it'd be safe.'

'That's right. Don't let him hang all the rap on you. At least you'll have company when they hang you, if you rat on him.'

'Don't worry, mister. Me and my mate'll tell all we know about that damned Farlow — he puts us up to this. I — ugh!'

He broke off, and simultaneously the Knight went flat on the ground. For he had heard the pop behind, and he had seen the way the flashy one had doubled up, hit by a slug in the chest. As the Knight groped in his pocket for his own revolver, he saw from the corner of his eye the unconscious burly man jump also, and cough, sending blood spattering from his lips.

The Knight had squirmed round, was staring keenly into the dark gardens. He thought he saw a brief glimpse of a white face in the shadows, then it was gone. But he knew then what had happened. Baron Blud must have followed him, must have overheard the conversation, and understood enough to know the capture of the crooks meant trouble for the cause he served. So he had removed the two killers, speedily and efficiently.

And he was still out there, lurking in the shrubbery! Or was he? He had no way of knowing that the two men he had killed had been after the plans. No one yet knew that except the man Knight had spoken to on the phone. No, decided the Knight, Blud could not possibly be aware of the fact that the plans were near at hand, or he would not have departed so easily — *if* he had departed.

It seemed clear what had transpired: Blud had been behind the Knight, had seen him enter the house, and had awaited events. He had then overheard the conversation, and when the flashy one had announced his intention of ratting — telling all he knew about Farlow — Blud had understood enough to see that would mean much trouble, and many questions from the police. Accordingly, he had killed the would-be squealers.

But why hadn't he risked a shot at the Knight? Or was he still around? Did he intend to?

The Knight cautiously groped his way towards the flashy man, got his hands to the man's shoulders, and gently eased him off the floor. Blud was apparently still among those present; his gun cork-popped savagely from the undergrowth, and a neat round hole traced itself on the already dead man's forehead.

'Fun and games,' murmured the Knight gently as he allowed the fleshy corpse to fall untidily to the floor again. 'That should produce the dear baron!'

He wormed his way back into the shadows, found security behind a porch standard, and eased his six-foot frame some inches upright, as quietly as a cat on a night marauding expedition.

There was silence; ten full minutes of it. And then Blud, or at least a dark figure whom the Knight took to be Blud, emerged from the shrubbery, and started stealthily along the path. Lance stood tight, shoulder to shoulder with shadow, as the figure advanced. He could see now that it was definitely Blud. That white face almost glimmered in the darkness.

The baron crept up the steps and stood above the corpses. Then he bent swiftly and began to run eager fingers through the pockets of the small man. As yet, he did not seem to have noticed the absence of the third dead man.

Blud was smiling sadistically as he searched; obviously his night's killing had been a pleasure to him. The Knight remembered with revulsion that Janis had said he was an evil, sadistic beast.

And then that temptation crept over the Knight again; the seat of Baron Blud's stove-pipe pants were again invitingly outspread before him, and his foot was itching.

Blud didn't even know what had hit him; and the Knight put all thirteen stone of beef and sinew into that kick. Blud was lifted willy-nilly from the step, shot into the air, and hefted into the garden, alighting with much uproar on the lawn.

The Knight was about to follow up his advantage when the sound of a car in the road outside, and the wide sweep of strong headlamps, held him motionless for a moment. Then there was no doubt — the car was about to turn into the drive of that very house. Probably the foreign minister returning from the ball. Blud had heard the car also, and he scurried frantically away into the bushes without a backward glance at his assailant. The Knight paused, undecided.

It would certainly be a severe shock to the dance-goers to return to such a scene of mayhem and mass murder. But the Knight knew if he was found there, the police would be very awkward about the whole thing. No, he could not afford to get into any scrapes at the moment.

As the car roared towards the front door, he vaulted lithely over the wall of the steps, into the garden, and round the house. Of Blud there was no sign. Even as the foreign minister made the discovery of the two corpses on his front porch and held up his wife, who thought the time ripe for a faint, the Knight was slithering through the shadows towards his apartments.

Before he went to bed, he telephoned Princess Janis and gave her a brief résumé of the night's events. He also requested her to give him an alibi, just in case — the alibi that he had been with her from six that evening, to half past one in the morning.

5

In Which Chief Inspector Floyd Enters

The Knight was at breakfast when his landlady knocked on the door and announced: 'A gentleman from Scotland Yard to see you, sir.'

'Ah,' said Lance. 'Is he the possessor of large flat feet and a weather-worn bowler? Is he as lean and lanky and miserable as a Tibetan monk? Does he smell of chewing tobacco?'

There was a silence while, seemingly, the landlady verified these points. Then she called: 'Yes, sir.'

'I was expecting him,' said the Knight with a smile. 'Come in, Chief Inspector Floyd — and don't forget to remove your bowler, will you?'

Floyd entered with a disconsolate expression on his face. He had brushed up against the Knight before, and had not yet learned to take that worthy's badinage in a spirit of composure. In fact, although outwardly he betrayed no emotion, inwardly he seethed and fermented whenever it fell to his lot to interview that airy gentleman who was suspected of so much and could be proved of so little.

He sat dourly in a chair and waited while the Knight forked the last morsel of kipper into his mouth. Then he said: 'You've put your foot in it this time, Knight.'

The Knight bestowed a tranquil smile on him and lit a thoughtful cigarette. 'I have? Tell me more, Ernest.'

Floyd glowered. The disrespectful use of his first name had a habit of irritating him intensely. Which was exactly why the Knight inevitably used it. 'Where were you between the hours of ten o'clock last night and two o'clock this morning?'

The Knight looked as if he was thinking back. 'Let's see now . . . if I'm not mistaken, I was in the company of a charming princess — quite charming. We got along rather well together.'

Floyd grunted with happiness. To him, the Knight was merely fencing for time.

Apparently he had no alibi ready, and that was just where Floyd had always wanted to catch him. Princess indeed!

'You better start telling the truth,' said Floyd, 'because I'm taking you in this time, Knight. On a murder charge. And if you try to tell the jury that you were with a princess, there's no doubt you'll hang. I thought you had more brains than to spin a silly story like that.'

'Thanks for the doubtful compliment,' the Knight said, sipping his coffee. 'Care for a cup of this? Good for keeping you awake — you need it, Inspector.'

Floyd scowled. 'You won't do yourself any good, Knight,' he said, 'by being funny. I've caught you this time without an alibi. But if you can't think up a better one on the spur of the moment than the tale you've told me, you'd better not try. If you were with a — a princess,' he sneered, 'where is she? Will she verify your story?'

'I expect she would.'

'What?' gasped Floyd, eyes protruding.

'But,' he went on sorrowfully, 'I wouldn't like to drag her into bad company. She's used to mixing with gentlemen, and if you chaps began chivvying her about, the poor woman would never recover from the shock. I mean, she's mixed with men who always remove their hats when in the house.' And he eyed the inspector's headgear with a pointed expression.

Floyd flushed and whipped off his hat. Then, doggedly, he stuck it back on his head, looking rather like a defiant child who had decided at the last minute that he was too old to be bossed about. He growled: 'We'll overlook my hat.'

'It'll be a strain,' said the Knight. 'It's such an unusual hat, but I'll try.'

'And get back to this — this princess,' snorted Floyd. 'If there is such a person — and I don't believe for a minute there is — either you have to get her to bear witness for you, or I'm taking you in without any further argument. See!'

'I'm sorry, Ernest,' apologised the Knight. 'It can't be done.'

'I didn't think it could,' gloated Floyd, triumphantly. 'This time you've gone off the rails once too often. I must say I never expected you to leave yourself without an alibi.'

'It can't be done,' went on Lance, 'because the lady is at present incognito.'

'And if that isn't the silliest pack of lies you ever told, I'll resign my job and pound a beat again,' rumbled Floyd.

'Then you'd better get your shoes soled and heeled, because it's quite true.'

'But yet you refuse to reveal the lady's name?'

The Knight waved the question aside airily. 'Suppose you tell me what I'm supposed to have done?'

Floyd nodded and began ticking items off on his fingers. 'One: you're under suspicion of murdering a man called Count Dornich at the home of the Lazanian ex-foreign minister, and ambassador to Britain. Two: you're also under suspicion of illegally entering enclosed premises to commit that deed. Three: you're suspected of killing two crooks, well known to the police, at the same address.'

'Is that all? You're sure I haven't blown up the Houses of Parliament, or stolen the crown jewels?'

'If anything like that did happen, I'd come to you first!'

'And by what masterly methods of deduction have you arrived at those conclusions?'

'It was a police constable who put us on the trail,' Floyd said. 'When he heard that there'd been a triple killing at eighty-three Gresham Terrace, he remembered a man stopping him late last night and asking him the address of the Lazanian minister in a roundabout sort of way. He reported that incident, and his description of the man fitted you exactly. I showed him some photographs of you, and he said it was dark at the time, but he was certain you were the man. Now, why did you want to know that particular address? And how is it that about the same time, three men were killed there?'

'I didn't want to know the address,' supplied the Knight. 'And as your constable says, it was dark last night, and he could have been mistaken. As it so happens, he was.'

Floyd fumed: 'Don't try to wriggle out

of this one. You won't manage it, by God!'

The Knight regarded him pityingly. 'Ernest, Ernest, I sometimes despair of you ever learning. You're one of the major cogs of a great and efficient police organisation. But when will you ever learn enough not to try to pin any murder that happens within twenty miles of my flat on me? Why not look for the real killer?'

'Don't give me any argument. If you can't produce this mythical princess of yours, I'm hauling you in and holding you on suspicion.'

The Knight looked at him long and hard. He knew that Floyd was thinking he'd got the Knight at last — congratulating himself on the way Lance had been bowled out, and quite sure that his alibi of a princess was purely imaginary. And the Knight hated to spoil that moment of supreme triumph for him. But he had to. He didn't wish to answer any police questions at the moment — he was far too busy.

He said: 'All right, Ernest. You win.'

'You'll come without trouble?'

'Come? Good heavens, no. I meant I'd

overlook my scruples about dragging the lady into contact with a policeman and take you to see her. She'll verify my story. And if the word of a constable stands up against that of a princess of integrity, I'll eat that moth-marked bowler of yours, Ernest!'

Floyd's jaw had dropped wildly. He knew the Knight was going to slip the net again. He knew the look in those daredevil steel-flecked eyes. It had happened so often before, and Floyd realised with a sickening certainty that it would happen often again. It was going to happen now. The Knight hadn't been telling bedtime stories — he had a princess! He had simply been leading Floyd up the garden path, stringing him along. Floyd knew he might as well call it a day there and then; he knew that if he accompanied the Knight, he was in for more ridicule — ridicule that would make his toes writhe in his boots. But he was a man who stuck to the bitter end, and stoically he plunged off to his fate.

He said: 'I'll come along with you,

then. But if you're trying to make a fool of me . . . '

'Is it possible?' said the Knight in some surprise; and leaving the outraged Yard man to figure that out, he went to change.

* * *

Colonel Mercer, a retired Indian army man on half pay, rose from his pruning and removed his glove to shade his eyes from the mid-morning sunshine while he peered towards the entrance gates of his large and comfortable residence.

Two men were walking up the drive, and their path would bring them practically on top of him. He did not know them. One was young dark and lean, with the physique and carriage of a sixteenth-century buccaneer; and his companion was tall, doleful and stringy, with large feet and a shiny bowler hat.

The colonel removed his hand from his grizzled features as they approached and stepped onto the pathway. He eyed them from faded blue eyes on which the burning Indian sun had taken its toll, and stepped forward politely to greet them.

'Good morning, gentlemen. Is there anything I can do for you? My name is Mercer — Colonel Mercer. I must apologise for my garb. I admit I look a little like the gardener at the moment.'

He smiled pleasantly and the Knight returned his smile. He said: 'I should like very much to see a young lady who is staying with you — Princess Janis of Lazania.'

Mercer started, and said quickly: 'I'm sorry — you must be mistaken.'

'It's quite all right,' said the Knight with a smile. 'She's expecting me, I think. I telephoned her before I came.'

'Oh, the call was from you? I see. The name is — '

'Lance Knight, and Chief Inspector Floyd of New Scotland Yard.'

The colonel shot a keen glance at the Inspector. 'I hope there isn't any trouble? Janis has said nothing to me.'

'No, there's no trouble,' said Floyd. 'Just a routine matter.'

Mercer nodded and vanished into the bushes. He was back almost at once with

Janis; her arm was linked affectionately through his own, and they were smiling and chatting.

Janis looked delightful in a flimsy summer frock, which clung to her delicious curves closely and rippled enchantingly with every step she took. Her face was gay and cool, her hair simply arranged. Anything less like a princess would have been hard to imagine. Once again, her bearing, graceful and regal, branded her as above the ordinary run of women. She stepped forward quickly when she saw the Knight and took his hand impetuously.

'Lance — I had your telephone call, but I can't imagine what on earth you want me to meet the inspector for.'

'To help me, Janis,' he responded. 'There seems to be some doubt as to where I was last night, from ten to two. I thought you could straighten that out, since Mr. Floyd appears to think I was roaming round London committing seven different kinds of skullduggery.'

'I'll take it from here,' said Floyd, stepping forward. 'I'm delighted to make your acquaintance, your highness. And if you can answer one or two straightforward questions, I won't trouble you any more.'

'Anything, Inspector, for you London policemen. I think you're wonderful!'

'Yes, hmm!' said Floyd, actually blushing. 'Thank you, your highness. We do our best.'

'Please call me Janis,' she said. 'I'm incognito here, and I get so tired of being thought different. I'm not, Inspector. I'm only a woman after all, you see.'

'Thank you, Miss Janis.' It was easy to see the inspector was charmed by her. He coughed and went on: 'I'd like you to tell me of your movements last night, if you will?'

'Certainly. I met Lance here about six and we went to Sylvester's to dine. We left there and went on to a public house nearby for a drink. Then we made for Claymore Ballroom and danced until about half-past eleven. We had a final nightcap at Lance's flat, and then drove back down here in the car. We didn't part at once; we sat in the car in the driveway, talking. It was half past two by the dashboard clock before Lance left.'

Floyd nodded forlornly and said: 'That seems clear enough, Miss Janis. I'd like someone to verify it. Not that I doubt your word, of course, but as a matter of official routine. Did anyone see you after ten together?'

She looked thoughtful. 'Lots of people must have done so. But I'm afraid no one who knew us.'

Colonel Mercer stepped forward. 'Perhaps I can help, Inspector. I heard the car drive up at about one-thirty last night and glanced through the window of the library, where I was studying a book on horticulture. I saw Janis and a young man in the car — and I feel sure, now the matter's been brought back to my mind, that it was this young, man. If not, the fellow was remarkably like him.'

Floyd nodded. 'Well, I think that's all. There won't be any need to take you along, Knight.'

Lance slapped his back. 'Poor old Floyd. He's been trying to arrest me for years, for everything from mass murder to stealing pennies from a blind man's money tin. Buck up, man. You may pull it off one of these days.'

'Oh, Inspector,' said Janis reproachfully, 'how could you ever think Lance would murder anyone? He wouldn't hurt a fly.'

'I don't suppose he would — he'd have no reason to,' said Floyd with a touch of his old acerbity. 'But it wasn't flies that were hurt last night, Miss Janis.'

She gave him a dazzling smile.

'But even if I haven't helped my case much by coming along, it's been worth it for the privilege of meeting you, miss.'

The Knight gazed at him admiringly. 'You're becoming quite an adept at the art of paying compliments, Inspector. Who'd have suspected that thoughts like that could possibly emanate from beneath that battered bowler?'

Floyd grinned good-humouredly. He had got over his disappointment now, and he did not feel so sore. The Knight had somehow — and he could not say how — persuaded the princess to stand an alibi for him. Floyd was quite sure the

Knight had been mixed up in the affair of last night. But what chance would a policeman, who had only seen his man hazily in the darkness, stand against a princess with a reputation who claimed to have spent a charming evening with him, and a retired colonel who backed her up? Floyd gave up and contented himself with the knowledge that there would be a next time when the Knight might not be so fortunate.

'I'll have to bustle back to town now,' he said. 'You coming, Knight?'

'Must you leave?' the colonel asked. 'I meant to ask you both to stay for lunch.'

'Sorry, but I can't,' Floyd said regretfully. 'I'd like to, but duty calls.'

'Fortunately I haven't any odious duties to perform,' said the Knight with a grin. 'I'll stay. And thank you, Colonel.'

The three watched Floyd, after he had taken his leave, trudging along the dusty lane towards the electric railway that would whirr him back to the busy city. When he was a speck in the distance, the colonel turned to Janis and said: 'Now what's all this, Janis?'

She blushed. 'Thanks ever so much for backing us up.' She gave his arm a squeeze. 'Lance is helping me to beat Farlow and his gang at their dirty work. Last night they tried to steal the plans for the oil wells — but although they killed poor Eric, Lance got the plans back.'

'You have them safe?' said the colonel, giving Lance a glance.

'Quite safe. No amount of searching will unearth them. I'd like to thank you also, Colonel, for your support.'

Mercer smiled. 'I knew Janis came home early last night and went to bed. But I also know that if she claimed to have been with you, she had a good reason for doing so. I know her father well; we were at Oxford together, and there's nothing I wouldn't do for his daughter.'

Lance said: 'I'm with you there, Colonel.'

6

In Which a Princess Becomes a Woman

Lance Knight had sincerely meant those words to the colonel, and he noticed Janis looking at him strangely as he said them. He couldn't quite place the look — whether it was gratitude, admiration, or something deeper; much deeper. He hoped that it was the latter, for no adventure was complete to him without a beautiful woman — and this particular adventure promised to fulfill all he required of it.

Lunch was a quiet affair, with the colonel yarning pleasantly of his school-days with the man who was now the deposed king of Lazania. Janis too, it came out, had been educated in England, and loved the country almost as much as she loved her own Lazania. Lunch over, the colonel went into the kitchen garden to bandy words with his dour head gardener, and Janis insisted that Lance should see the rose garden.

Sunshine, the smell of hay from a neighbouring field, and the sweet subtle scent of roses made a perfect setting for her simple yet dignified beauty. And looking at her profile, calm and cool, Lance wondered if she ever became as other women were — ever forgot she was a princess and became plainly and solely, woman.

She looked at him suddenly, for long minutes. They were seated in a bower among the roses, and not a sound was to be heard except for the tweeting of the birds nearby and the voices of colonel Mercer and his head gardener, disputing whether or not the tea roses should be cut. But all that was far away; and here another world existed; a world in which purity and sweetness reigned, and people like Korvin, Blud and Farlow were non-existent.

She broke the long silence at last with a simple question: 'What are you thinking of, Lance?'

He had been studying his feet, but now

he looked up at her and smiled. 'Princesses.'

'Any in particular?'

'One — a very charming one. I was wondering if they felt the way other women feel.'

'In what way?' she asked, slowly and softly.

He shrugged. 'I don't know. Forget it.'

She smiled and didn't press the point. 'I can't ever thank you enough for what you've done. Poor Eric — he died for Lazania, and I know he'd be happy to think you were working for the same end, too. But what are we going to do now, Lance?'

He took her hand and held it, and she made no attempt to withdraw it. He said: 'Leave it to me. For your part, just try to find out the country Count Dornich was trying to persuade to intercede. When you've found them, you take over the job where he left off. Can you do that?'

'With the help of Costan Dervent — he's the ex-foreign minister of Lazania; the man with whom Eric was staying when he was murdered. He's charming, and he'll do anything he can to restore the old rule to Lazania.'

'Good. Then you fix up that end of it, while I concentrate on Farlow and Blud.'

'But my parents — my family?'

'While I have the plan and you don't know where it is, they can't hold you responsible for not obtaining it. And in any case, there's still three weeks before the worst could happen, and before that time is up I hope to get somewhere.'

Her fingers stirred in his hand, and a thrill ran along him. She gazed up at him, so helplessly, so dependently, with a mysterious look deep in her eyes. He could not resist the madness that took him in its grip, and he bent over, pulling her to him with a strong arm, and pressed his lips to hers.

She was passive for only a second; and then he knew she was returning the kiss; was pressing her cool, curved body against him, and was looking at him with all her soul and heart in her eyes. At last she detached herself from him, laughed a little self-consciously, and adjusted her hair where it had been disarranged.

'Does that answer your question about whether a princess can become like other women?' He nodded, without speaking. She went on: 'There isn't very much princess in me, Lance. I'm almost all woman.' Then she was silent, and preoccupied with her thoughts. 'Lance,' she said awkwardly at length, 'you won't place too serious a construction on — on what just happened?'

'No,' he said mechanically. 'It was — part of the adventure.'

She nodded, but didn't seem very happy about it. There was an awkwardness upon them both now; a feeling of unreality that this couldn't have happened; that a kiss couldn't have had such an effect upon them. Surely they weren't both so susceptible?

Lance said suddenly: 'Why shouldn't I place a serious side on that kiss, Janis? You meant it. I meant it.'

'No,' she said almost desperately. 'No, you mustn't, Lance. It would never work out. I — I have to think of Lazania. I'm next in line to the throne.'

'But I understood you had a brother?'

'I have. But you don't understand. In my country, succession goes always to the eldest, irrespective of sex. And — and my marriage has already been arranged — to Prince Paul of Lebania, a richer neighbouring country. It is vital that I should marry Paul.'

He said tonelessly: 'I thought you were all woman a moment ago. Now you're all princess!'

'I'm not, Lance. But I'm thinking of my — my duty.'

He snapped out of his mood and stood up with a grin. 'Congratulations, anyway. What's he like, this Paul?'

'He's nice — young and agreeable.'

'You love him?'

'No, I don't. And I'm sure he doesn't love me, for that matter. But that doesn't make any difference, Lance.'

He grinned again. 'I've read of that sort of thing in novels. I didn't think it happened in real life. Nor did I think you'd be such a stickler for duty.'

There were almost tears in her eyes, and her head was cast down. 'I have to do it, Lance, can't you see? Lebania is a powerful country, and several times in the past it has been on the verge of declaring war on Lazania over territorial disputes. If they did, we wouldn't stand a chance. We'd fall under their invasion. But if I marry Paul, that will cement us. And not only will we be safe from any further attacks and threats, but also we'll have their protection in the event of anything happening again.'

'Then why don't they extend a bit of protection now?'

'Why should they? We're not tied to them yet. Their prince is not yet the prince consort of Lazania.'

He took her hands again and smiled down at her. 'Let's make a pact, and keep it. For the rest of our adventure, let's remain to each other just unattached people — plain Janis Smith, and plainer Lance Knight.'

'No, Lance. We'd only hurt ourselves more when we did have to part.'

'Well, why not? We'll get over that. And it would make this the one outstanding adventure of them all. It would be perfect. When the time to split up did roll round, at least we'd have had a few days — hours — with each other, as ordinary people.'

'But — but how would you want me to act? How would you want me to be to you?'

'Just be yourself. Not as Princess Janis, heir to the throne, but a Janis Smith — ordinary everyday woman. You will agree to that?'

'Do I have to, to get you to go on helping me?'

'Good heavens, of course you don't. I didn't mean anything like that. I've pledged myself to lend you a hand, and I won't break my word — count on it. I'm sorry you feel like that about it. I didn't realise it might have seemed to you I was blackmailing you into something you didn't want. Let's just forget it.'

She stood up, wound one arm about his neck, and said: 'No, Lance! I didn't mean to say that. Of course I'll be plain Janis Smith until the end of the adventure. I want to be.'

'You may be Janis Smith,' he said,

holding her tightly, 'but you'll never be plain!'

He knew she'd be hurt at the end of it all — knew he would, too. But, as he said, a few hours . . . days . . .

★   ★   ★

Lance Knight slammed on a dark wide-brimmed hat, slid a small revolver into his pocket, clicked off the flat lights, and left the building. He walked quickly and quietly through London until he reached the point where Farlow's home was located. As he had done the previous evening, he scaled the wall silently, walked arm in arm with the shadows round the long lawn, and brought up against the window.

The French window was ajar, and inside the room Baron Blud was talking to Farlow, and seeming to have some trouble making himself understood. 'How I know he got plans?' Blud was grating, thumping the table.

'No, you couldn't have known, could you? But when you followed him to the

Lazanian ex-ambassador's home, you might have realised something funny was going on.'

'Pah!' snorted Blud. 'I do not think he got plans. How do I to know this?'

'Well,' said Farlow, 'the boss has rung me up to tell me he's got the plans. Now you're supposed to get them from him. In fact, if the steps I've already taken to find it don't work out, you'll have to see what you can do about killing him — but not until you know where the plans are, mind. You understand?'

'I kill — but first find plans.'

'Right. I've got someone watching his flat, and the moment he leaves it now, it will be searched.'

Lance grinned in the darkness to himself. He didn't mind having his flat searched. If the searchers found the plans there he would be very surprised — far more surprised than they would be.

Farlow went on: 'If that fails, you'll have to find him, and we'll force it out of him. We must have those plans at once, or some other power may walk in and throw Korvin and his bandits out. That would mean you'd be out of a job. I wonder where the devil is! I know his record — and I know he won't drop the affair until he's either been killed or got the better of us. Ten to one he's got some scheme up his sleeve.'

'You're right, Sebastian, I have,' said the Knight, walking casually into the room and parking on the arm of a chair nearby. 'Good evening, Baron. I notice you don't seem able to sit down yet.'

Blud and Farlow stared, petrified. They were unable to credit their senses; unable to believe that Daniel could be so foolhardy as to walk into the lion's den. What they didn't realise was that in the Knight's opinion, they were very far from being lions, or anywhere near that status. He regarded them purely as rats; big rats, but still rats.

He proceeded at once to enlighten them to that opinion by saying: 'I thought I'd pop along to your rat hole to have a word or two about the plans you seem so anxious to get your paws on, brothers. A nice, cozy little chat.'

Farlow nodded to Blud, who began to

move round the room towards the window. The Knight watched him with interest, and saw him close and stand against the windows aggressively; saw him draw his silenced revolver.

Farlow crossed to the door, warily watching the Knight, turned the key in the lock, and slipped it in his pocket. Then he sneered: 'I didn't think you'd be fool enough to put yourself in our hands. But if you think you're going to leave this house before we know what you've done with those plans, you're mistaken.'

'The plans? Oh, yes, that scrap of paper I took from a somewhat untidy corpse last night. Let me see — I think I lit my cigarette with it.'

Farlow growled: 'Indeed? And I think you didn't. Unless you tell us where those plans are, you won't be leaving this house. That's final!'

'That's a pity,' said Lance sadly. 'He'll be so disappointed.'

'He? Who?'

'The plainclothes gentleman with flat feet who followed me here, as he thought, unobserved. If I don't come out he'll get anxious, and phone Scotland Yard as he has doubtless been instructed. Then just where would you two be?'

'You're lying.'

'Not at all. Chief Inspector Floyd is firmly convinced I know a lot more than I admit about the murders last night. He's had a man on my tail ever since I returned to town this evening. If you don't believe that, take a look from the front door. Unless I'm mistaken, you'll spot a sturdy-looking gent, attired in regulation Derby, standing guard at the corner of the street and watching the wall where I went over, and also the front door.'

Without a word, Farlow left the room, leaving Blud to look after the Knight. He was back again in no time, his face a little pale. He said: 'He's telling the truth. There is a man watching there.'

'I kill him?' said Blud, licking his lips eagerly, but Farlow shook his head angrily.

'No, you don't, damn it. You did too much killing last night for my liking. I don't want to hang for the sake of these oil wells.' He turned his attention to the Knight and rasped: 'Well, we've got the drop on you this time, Knight. But since you've been followed, it isn't going to do us much good, is it?'

'No, it isn't,' agreed the Knight. 'You didn't think I'd be foolish enough to walk in on you gentlemen unless I knew you'd have to let me go again, did you?'

'What did you come for?'

The Knight smiled. 'I came to warn you that since only I know where the plans are hidden, it would be foolish to attempt to torture Princess Janis's parents — very foolish. I'd take a very stern view of anything of that nature, Farlow. I don't know who sends the orders to Lazania, but I expect it's either you or Baron Bluddy — sorry, Blud. And I'd like you to know as a matter of interest that if one hair of their heads is harmed, I'll personally undertake to wipe the precious pair of you from the face of the globe. No one could blame me for that, since you've infested it quite long enough.'

'Is that all you came for?' said Farlow, and the Knight knew by his subdued tone that at least he was afraid.

He said: 'Yes. Isn't that enough?'

'Suppose we wipe you out, first?'

'You can try; plenty have already. If you manage it you'll be the very first, Sebby. Frankly I don't think you have the guts of a louse, and your heathenistic friend there hasn't got the brains of a gnat. Between you, you might cook something up. But I think that any fun will be inspired by the man over you, and not you yourselves. You can tell that man from me that I firmly intend to find him; and when I do, I have every intention of playing the funeral march on his front teeth, with my gun. I think that's all for now; don't let me overstay my welcome. Unless you'd care to make sure the plans aren't on me before I leave?'

Farlow shook his head, upon which reposed a large round bump and a wad of cotton wool and sticking plaster. 'No; you wouldn't suggest that if you had the plans with you. We can wait.'

'Bit cagey, eh?' said the Knight with a grin. 'Frightened of a repetition of last night's fireworks? Bet you thought you were in a planetarium after that bump on the noggin. Just how many stars did you see, Sebby?'

Farlow grunted. 'I didn't count them. But nothing like the amount *you'll* see one of these days, Knight.'

The Knight smiled and got up. He looked at Baron Blud, who had been trying to follow the drift of the conversation. 'You'll be able to explain to our corpse-faced friend what I've said when I've gone, won't you? I wouldn't like him to miss any of it, you know. I'm a firm believer in kindness to dumb animals, and he looks so pathetic standing there with his mouth open.'

Farlow unlocked the door, and Baron Blud snarled and started from his position. Farlow rapped: 'No good. Let him go. Police outside.'

Blud relaxed, puzzled. He was in the awkward position of having to rely on Farlow for information and instructions in a country that was strange and new to him. Lance walked from the house unmolested and strode rapidly towards the bowler-hatted merchant standing by the street lamp at the corner. He slid a ten-shilling note into his hand and said: 'Five bob each way, Carter's Folly in the three o'clock, Sam. And here's a quid for yourself for your trouble.'

'What trouble, mister?' asked the bewildered bookmaker, who was hanging round waiting for his regulars to place their bets.

'Never mind what trouble.' Lance grinned. 'But if anyone should roll out of that house and look at you as if you're a policeman, try and pretend you are, will you? Good chap.'

'Policeman? Hell! I hate 'em.'

'Mutual. Good night, Sam.'

With a low laugh, the Knight had gone; and for the entire rest of that evening, Farlow was quite unable to understand why the plainclothes man hadn't followed Lance Knight home again!

Meanwhile, Lance was striding along, whistling merrily. He felt he had not gained much by his visit; but he also knew Farlow would not have the nerve to order any torturing of Janis's family in the face of the Knight's stern warning.

He knew Farlow; knew what a yellow-belly he was.

He was thinking of Blud, and wondering just how far that worthy would go to achieve his ends. Had Farlow a great deal of control over the sadist? Or was Farlow merely his guide, so to speak, advising him, but having no actual power to direct his course?

Still wondering, Lance walked into his rooms — and bumped into the woman who was just walking out!

7

In Which Things Happen

The woman was quite astonishingly beautiful; and even the Knight, who counted himself an expert on the quality of women's looks, had to admit that she had something the others hadn't. Hers was not the beauty of Janis — she had the same exotic quality, but lacked the purity and simplicity. Yet her beauty was even more outstanding than Janis's, in a dark, daring manner. She was a woman of the world, and every line of her suggested hidden delights; every movement fierce, straining passions.

The negligée she was wearing was charming, and apparently of Parisienne design. It was slit slightly on the left side, allowing a firm white limb to escape its diaphanous folds. An entrancing limb! Having taken all this in, the Knight said: 'Now what am I meant to do? Cheer?'

She betrayed no alarm apart from a momentary narrowing of her exquisite velvety eyes. 'That depends. What do you usually do when you find young ladies in your bedroom?'

'That would depend on whether they were there by arrangement or accident. But I don't usually find young ladies in such a compromising position.'

She made no attempt to get out; instead she selected a cigarette from his case on the table, and gallantly he lit it for her.

He said: 'I have to admit you're rather a cool customer,' and she smiled back at him.

'You aren't exactly prone to hysterics yourself, are you?'

The Knight sat on the settee and patted the cushion beside him. 'Sit down. I can see this ripening into a beautiful friendship, or what have you. What's your name?'

'Marcia — Marcia Jones.'

'Dear me, is it really? What an extraordinary number of Smiths and Joneses I'm cannoning into these days. I suppose it'll be Browns next.'

'That isn't my real name, of course. A young lady doesn't give her real name when caught in a young gentleman's bedroom, does she?'

'I think not. Actually, you aren't English at all, are you?'

She started. 'What makes you think that?'

'Your inflection. I happen to know a young lady who has the same trait in her words — she comes from Lazania.'

The woman shook her head. Emphatically. 'I'm afraid it must be pure coincidence. I'm perfectly English.'

He nodded, went as far as the sideboard, and poured drinks. Then he turned round. 'Well, did you find what you were looking for?'

'I don't understand you.'

'They never do. But try hard. What I should have said was, did you find the plans?'

She took the drink and sipped delicately, looking him full in the eyes, her oval face set into a little smile. 'I still don't understand you. But I expect you think you have a right to know why I'm here. And I'll tell you. I rent the flat above this one — '

'I've not seen you before. When did you move in?'

'Only today. I spotted you going out tonight, and soon afterwards I happened to see, from the head of the stairs, two men entering your rooms. They were furtive and stealthy about it, and I didn't know quite what to do, so I waited. They were in here about ten minutes, and when they came out again, I overheard one say to the other: 'Well, he hasn't left it in there! We'd better get going.''

'So you hurried down, very thoughtfully, to see what they'd been up to?'

'That's true, Mr. Knight.'

'You know my name?'

'Why, er, yes. I — I've heard of you.'

She was holding her hand to her breasts firmly; it might have been a nervous gesture, but it didn't seem nervous. The Knight didn't think she was a nervous type, either. He stood up, crossed to her, jerked her to her feet, and pulled her hand away from the top of her negligée. A small queerly shaped metal instrument fell from beneath the hem, and he stooped and picked it up.

He said: 'Do you always make a habit of carrying such a useful little tool as a skeleton key in the neck of your negligée?'

She flushed and took it from his hands, then sat down again. 'Really, you're rather uncouth, Mr. Knight.'

'Aren't I?' he agreed. He went on, while she was silent: 'If I just tell you why you're here, and you tell me if I'm right, that will satisfy me. I presume you came for the plans of the Lazanian oil wells?'

She nodded; she was recovering her poise.

'Naturally you didn't find them — but I'd expected something of this sort, from a conversation I heard between your charming employer Farlow and his pug-ugly assistant Baron Blud. Mind you . . . ' he went on, glancing round, 'I admit you're a very neat searcher. You've put everything back in its correct position, as far as I can see, for which I must confess I'm grateful.'

'Have I? Wait until you see your study,

Mr. Knight.' She accepted another drink and looked at him as he lay back on the settee with his glass, idly twirling it by the stem. 'Mr. Knight, I don't know where you've hidden those plans, but we must have them.'

'You must?'

'We must. My father will be thrown out of — ' She stopped suddenly and bit her lip.

But it was too late. He eased upright and looked at her again. 'You were saying?'

'Nothing. A — a slip of the tongue.'

'Why not come clean? You were about to say your father would be thrown out of power, weren't you? And my guess is that your real name is Korvin. Is that right?'

'Well, what if I am Marcia Korvin? I'm helping my father — it isn't crime. It's politics.'

'Not what *you're* doing, isn't. I don't like lovely ladies who tangle in this kind of thing. I find they're much worse than the homely variety. Their beauty gets them places too fast. I'd say, at a guess, that you're very fond of that father of yours.'

'I am,' she said sullenly. 'Why else do you think I'd have agreed to risk my neck?'

'Money. Power. But assuming you're fond of him, it's only natural to say he's fond of you, also?'

'He is. And if anything happens to me — '

'Nothing will happen if you cooperate. But if you don't, things are going to be very unpleasant. For the time being, I'm going to keep you here.'

'Here?'

'Just that. I'm afraid I'll have to tie you up and pop you in a cupboard in my bedroom, and that won't be very nice. But I'll let you out into my rooms for a walk morning and evening, and I'll feed you well.'

'You're mad. I'll be missed.'

'You won't. For the simple reason that you're going to write a note to Farlow telling him you're hot on the trail of the plans, and will communicate again soon. When you've done that, you're going to write to your esteemed father, who I trust is as fond of you as you declare. You are going to inform him that if any of the Lazanian royal family are harmed while in captivity, the same treatment will be dished out to you. You will tell him the only way to secure your release is by sending the royal family — lock, stock, and whatever else there is — to safety in some neutral country. That done, you'll be released unharmed.'

'You can't do that — Farlow will hear from father, and he'll come here looking for me.'

'By which time you will no longer be here at all. I shall take steps to smuggle you out tonight or tomorrow, to a place of safety.' He went on: 'I'm going to have to tie you up, now. You'd be wise not to resist.'

He was ready for her when she came at him, kicking and clawing. He fought her off, but her fingernails raked down his face, her smooth body rippling fiercely against his own. He thrust her away; but she wriggled in again, and her fingers made claws and reached out for his eyes.

The Knight, sighing regretfully, dodged backwards, and clipped his right forward smoothly. She took it on the chin and slumped to the floor soundlessly. He picked her up and laid her on the settee. While she was out, he quickly roped her securely with the window cords, leaving only her right hand free from the elbow.

It was a full ten minutes before her eyes flickered open, and for a second her stare was blank. Then she raged: 'You hit me! I'll kill you for that!'

'I doubt it.' Her gaze followed him as he crossed to a writing desk. 'Just lie still whilst I obtain paper and pen ... We'll start with the letter to your father first. And if you refuse?' He patted the pocket where his gun was concealed. 'Let's just say I'm not afraid to use this on a would-be burglar.'

* * *

The large closed car drew up that same night outside the Knight's apartments. He had, on second thoughts, decided it would be safer to move Marcia at once.

110

And he was putting that scheme into immediate operation. With an invisible gag clamped in her mouth, she was hustled down the stairs rapidly, through the door, and into the car.

The Knight climbed behind the wheel, slotted in his gears, and sped out of London, through the quieter districts. He was heading for the little place at Land's End he had mentioned once to Farlow. It was early morning before they reached their destination, but at last they roared onto a large chalk cliff-top, and he drew up.

Two hundred feet and more below, the waves pounded wildly against the jagged spurs of rock, and against the face of the cliff. Dawn was breaking, and a flight of gulls circled squawking above the sea, their eerie cries echoing through the loneliness of the spot.

The Knight pointed to a small stone cottage almost at the edge of the cliff and said: 'I've decided this will be safer for you. Added to which, it won't be as uncomfortable as the cupboard in my flat, which you seem to dislike so intensely.'

'You — you aren't leaving me alone here?'

'For a few hours. But then I'll arrange for a friend of mine to come along and feed you. I'm afraid you won't be able to have your bonds removed just yet, though.'

'You can't leave me here — alone,' she pleaded. 'There may be prowlers about.'

'You needn't worry. You'll notice there's only one room to the cottage, and that both windows are barred. The door is of solid oak on a steel plate, and once it's locked, no one could break in. No, you'll be perfectly safe here.'

'You'll be sorry for this, Knight,' she told him. 'My father may do as you order him now, but afterwards . . . '

'I'll take my chances,' said the Knight with a grin. 'Afterwards, I doubt very much whether your father will be long in power.'

He picked her up and carried her inside, where he made her comfortable in a deep armchair. 'I've used this place before for this purpose — that's why I bought it. It's ideal. Nor will it do any good to shout for help when I remove your gag. The nearest village is five miles away, and the roar of the surf would drown your cries. So for the present — pleasant dreams, Miss Korvin!'

8

In Which We Meet a Frightened Gentleman

Lance Knight took the driveway on two wheels and screamed up to brake before the door of Colonel Mercer's home. It was still early morning, but already the Colonel was pottering about his gardens, and he hurried across as his eyes fell on Lance.

'Good morning, Mr. Knight. It's nice to see you again, and I know Janis will be pleased. Eh?'

'Thank you, Colonel. Is she up yet?'

'Afraid not. But I'll ask the maid to call her, and meanwhile perhaps you'll have a bite of breakfast with me in the morning room.'

'Thanks, I will. I'm starving.'

They were finishing off the grilled kidneys when Janis came down, looking radiantly lovely as ever. Lance stood up and smiled at her, and she gave him her hand.

'Have you just come along on a visit, Lance?'

'No, not quite. I wondered if you'd care to lend a hand in the game. There won't be any danger.'

'Why, I'd love to. What do you want me to do?'

'Act as guard to a certain young lady . . . a Miss Marcia Korvin of Lazania.'

'M — Marcia Korvin? But . . . '

'You thought she was in Lazania with her father? Well, she isn't. She's here, and she's my prisoner.'

'But how?'

'It was simple. I just walked into my room last night and there she was, skimpily attired and caught red-handed. I found out who she was, and that she'd been searching for the plans — and I thought if we could threaten her father with her, he wouldn't dare touch your family. Far as I can see, her father thinks a great deal of her.'

'He does. I liked her myself at one time, but she turned just as violently as her father did; I was awfully disappointed.'

'Then you haven't any objections to running along to Land's End and keeping an eye on her?'

'No, none at all.'

'Good, then that's settled. I'll give you the keys before I leave, and you'll take my car down with you. Stay in the cottage as much as you can until you hear from me. Don't let her get her hands free, just in case she takes it into her head to try funny tricks. In the meantime, I'll get in touch with Korvin through Farlow and tell him that his daughter is a prisoner, and will only be released if and when your own folks are released — unharmed — and sent to safety.'

'Do you want me to go at once?'

'The moment you've had breakfast.'

She nodded and sat down to eat.

He went on: 'How are you making out with your plans for the intercession of some next-door power?'

'Wonderfully,' she said. 'Lebania is in touch with Costan Dervent, the ex-foreign minister, and they have almost

decided to intervene on our behalf —
with, of course, the promise of handsome
oil concessions.'

'That's fine. But until they do step in,
we'll just have to go on playing it the hard
way. Don't forget — take no chances with
Miss Korvin. I wouldn't like anything to
happen to you, but you're the only one I
can trust at the moment.'

Colonel Mercer, who had been sitting
drinking coffee, now said: 'You're quite
sure it will be safe? I would hate anything
to happen to Janis.'

'It can't be anything other than safe,'
said Lance. 'No one but the three of us
knows where the woman has been taken.
No one yet knows even that she's been
kidnapped. They've got that still to find
out.'

'I suppose it is,' he agreed, nodding.
'But I wouldn't forgive myself if anything
happened to Janis.'

'Nothing will. She'll be all right,
provided she doesn't give Miss Korvin
too much rope.'

'Oh, don't worry so, Colonel,' said
Janis with a smile. 'I'm quite old enough

to handle a little thing like this now.'

The colonel smiled and patted her shoulder kindly.

Lance said: 'If anything crops up, and you want to get in touch with me at once, telegraph my London address and I'll arrange to have any wires forwarded to me during the day, as far as possible. We have to wait a while now, until Korvin decides what he will do. But I feel he'll let your parents go. Or at least, not harm them.'

Janis waited until Colonel Mercer had gone back to the garden, then said: 'Lance, you're wonderful. How can I ever repay you for taking so much trouble for me?'

He took her in his arms and said softly: 'Be plain Janis Smith again, for a few minutes.'

*   *   *

The Knight yawned inelegantly, shifted the position of his feet where they rested on the opposite armchair, and eased the stance of his body against the one his long, lean muscularity was relaxing in.

He laid aside the copy of *Esquire* he was reading and lit a cigarette; he turned down the shade of the reading lamp so that it directed the beam of light over towards the door in a small pool. The footsteps he had heard ascending the stairs paused outside his door, and there was a knock.

'Come in,' called the Knight.

Farlow entered, with Baron Blud close behind him. He walked over nervously until he was centrally in the light pool, and in answer to a snapped order, halted.

'Don't move, either of you,' the Knight told them. 'I've got a gun trained on you from here, and I won't need two excuses to use it.'

Farlow rasped: 'You said you had a proposition to put to us — you asked us over here. Well, we're here. What's your proposition? Have you had the sense to see you should sell us those plans at last?'

'Hardly that,' said the Knight with a smile. 'Those plans are safe where only I know about them. No, I've come to the conclusion that I'll let you get in touch with Korvin and tell him that a certain letter he'll receive by air-mail is really from his daughter.'

'His — his daughter?'

'Precisely. Marcia Korvin. You needn't look startled, Farlow. You knew she was over here for those plans, didn't you? Of course. Only, she hadn't quite the knack of subterfuge, and I twigged who she was in next to no time. She is now in my hands, and a letter is on its way to Korvin informing him of that happy state of affairs. The idea is for him to release the Lazanian royal family, when his daughter will be released in turn by me. Failing that, I mean to hold her as hostage until I'm sure he hasn't harmed any of his prisoners, and doesn't intend to do so.'

Farlow growled: 'Where do we come in?'

'You can be invaluable by explaining to him that the letter is no forgery, and that Miss Korvin is hidden away in a safe place. Tell him you've seen me, and if anything happens to the king, queen, or any of their children, his daughter will suffer for it.'

Farlow said: 'You can take it from me that won't make any difference to Korvin. He's as hard as nails.'

'You'll tell him just the same. I've heard differently.'

'Sure, I'll tell him. But it won't help you any. Get a bit of sense, Knight, and turn over the plans. If you do that, Korvin will exile the royal family from Lazania, and that'll be an end of it.'

'I doubt it. He'd have the sense to know that as long as any heirs to the Lazanian throne are alive, there'd be constant danger of a revolution. Personally I think when he can no longer make use of them, he'll have them beheaded, or whatever other equally pleasant little method they adopt in that charming country.'

Farlow shrugged his shoulders. 'Is that all?'

'That's all. Don't forget to verify that letter for him.'

'I'll do that; but I'll take a bet that we'll have Miss Korvin back in our hands before a few days are out.'

'What makes you think that, Sebby?'

asked the Knight with interest.

'Never mind what makes me think it. I've got my reasons.'

The Knight yawned. 'I thought I'd let you boys know I hadn't been idle. Good night.'

'I'm asking you for the last time,' grunted Farlow.

'Good night! Shut the door after you — and take your tame vampire with you, will you?'

Farlow gave it up and stalked out, followed by Baron Blud, who had failed to pick out most of the conversation. The Knight turned up the reading lamp again, picked up the copy of *Esquire*, and read on.

His main desire in calling Farlow and Blud had been to see how they would react to the news that Miss Korvin had been captured. Their reaction had been disappointing; apparently they didn't care a goddamn whether she had been captured or not. To them she didn't count.

He read for almost an hour, then yawned again. He had missed sleep direly the previous night through driving Marcia Korvin down to her prison, and he was feeling the need for it. It was only half past nine by the clock on the mantelpiece, but Lance decided to take to his bed, and accordingly locked his door.

He was asleep instantly, sending mild snores echoing through the room; but from long experience he slept with one eye almost open, so that the slightest sound would awaken him.

It did.

The clock outside was chiming ten-thirty when he jerked upright in his bed and sat tight. He heard the sound again, coming from the other room, and defined it as a soft, urgent knocking at the flat door.

He slithered easily from his bed, shot his feet into slippers, and blotted out his taste in pajamas under a coarse dressing robe. He moved towards the bedroom door and through it to the flat door. His hand was actually on the knob and the key when a soft, throaty gasp and gurgle reached his ears from beyond.

Then the door was opened — and the

body of a tall thin man in evening dress collapsed weakly, face forward, at his feet.

He stepped into the corridor, on the alert; the place seemed entirely deserted. He ran swiftly to either end but failed to see any sign of intruders. He returned to the injured man.

It was a strain to lift him on to the bed, but he managed it. Then with skilful fingers, he gently extracted the long, ugly knife from the man's back and plugged the wound. He reached for a phone and put through a call to the nearest emergency hospital.

'Accident, yes. Send an ambulance right away. Stab wound.'

He hung up and forced a trickle of brandy between the man's teeth, which were tightly clenched. The thin man groaned and tried to roll over from his stomach to his back. The Knight said: 'Take it easy, whoever you are. There's an ambulance on the way.'

The man strained his face painfully half-sideways so that he could look at the Knight. He whispered haltingly: 'Are — are you — the — man they call — the

Knight? Lance Knight?'

Knight nodded, still holding the victim flat on his front. 'You were looking for me?'

'Ye — yes,' gulped the man. Then he stopped talking while he retched violently. Recovering, he went on: 'S-sorry. The bed . . . '

'Never mind the bed. How did this happen?'

'I came — came home from friends, tonight. There were two men lurking — in — in the shadows of my driveway; I didn't see them very clearly, but one had a very white face.'

'Blud — and, I expect, Farlow.'

'They — they seemed to think I might know where the plans to — to the Lazanian oil fields were hidden. I don't, of course; but they told me unless I forgot all about this scheme to persuade Lebania to step in and restore the old rule to Lazania, they'd — kill me.'

'Then you're Costan Dervent, the ex-foreign minister of Lazania?'

'And — and ambassador to Britain.' He nodded feebly.

'Go on, Mr. Dervent. What happened then?'

'They — they handled me roughly, but eventually they decided I really didn't know where the plans were. Then they warned me not to go to the police, and not to mention the incident to any one at all. After they had gone — or after I thought they had — I decided to get in touch with you. Princess Janis had already advised me to do so if any need for help arose. I started to walk here, and had the feeling all the time that I was being followed. I'd just reached your door, and — I — you see . . . '

He broke off, and a spasm of agony contorted his dark face; the skin grew white and taut; blood flecked his lips.

Lance Knight felt him grow stiff in his arm, and he laid him down gently, hearing subconsciously the banshee-howl of the ambulance siren in the street. He picked up the telephone again and said into it: 'Is that the Blestock Emergency Hospital? I'm sending your ambulance back without a passenger. What? No, I won't require it later. No. Scotland Yard will attend to all the details like that.'

There was a knock at the door; the ambulance attendants came in. Lance said: 'He's on the bed, poor devil. Take a look at him, but I think you'll find there's nothing anyone can do now.'

An intern took a look; he only needed the merest glance, then he turned back, said: 'The knife must have entered the right edge of the heart, far as I can say. How did it happen?' He looked curiously at Lance.

'How do these things always happen? He was mixed up in something he never thought would lead to his own murder.'

'Murder?' gasped the intern, backing away.

'I said murder. If you're interested, Scotland Yard will be along shortly. I'm about to telephone them.' He picked up the phone, gave the number, and said resignedly: 'Can I get in touch with Chief Inspector Floyd . . . ?'

It took some time, but he was lucky enough to contact Floyd just as he had been about to leave for home. Knight said: 'Ernest? This is a serious matter

— there's been murder done.'

'What?'

'Murder. A man been stabbed in the heart a few minutes ago.'

'Is — is he dead?' yelped Floyd.

'Would it be murder if he wasn't?' asked the Knight irritably.

'When — I mean how — what's your address?'

The Knight gave it him. Floyd continued: 'That address seems familiar — what's the name?'

'The name,' said the Knight tolerantly, 'is Lance Knight.'

There was a muffled groan from the other end, and Floyd said: 'My God! I was afraid it was you. Hold on, I'll be right over!'

Floyd arrived like an emaciated whirlwind some ten minutes later. He brought with him a police van, two detectives, two fingerprint men, a photographer, and the divisional surgeon. He bustled frantically round the room, shooting out questions like minute guns, and peering keenly at nothing in particular. He allowed the handcuffs in his pocket to jingle menacingly, and looked at the Knight as he did so.

At last he said: 'Well, why did you do it this time?'

'I've told you what happened. Don't be deliberately annoying,' said Lance, sitting on the edge of the bed by the corpse.

'Why,' barked Floyd, accusingly, 'did you kill this man?'

'If you insist, I'll tell you; because he had something I badly wanted.'

'He did? What?' said Floyd triumphantly.

'A gold watch and chain,' Lance told him.

The chief inspector scowled ferociously. 'Are you deliberately trying to be awkward, Knight?'

'No more than you are yourself. You don't think I'd be ass enough commit a perfectly good murder, then telephone you to come along and collect the corpse and snap the bracelets on me, do you?'

'I don't know what you'd do. That's the trouble. You're such a funny cuss.'

'Well, I didn't, anyway. The whole thing happened just as I told you.'

'Dervent? Was that his name?'

'It was. Costan Dervent, ambassador to Britain for Lazania.'

'That's the man who reported three killings at his home only the other day or so,' howled Floyd. 'Why didn't you tell me before?'

'You didn't give me the chance. You were too busy trying to find out why I'd done it. But if you'd only listen to me a minute, I'll tell you my theory — although I can't prove it. Costan Dervent was threatened only tonight. And I believe he was later followed here, and killed by the same person, in order to quieten him and frame me. And that man's name is Baron Blud.'

9

In Which the Knight Steps Out

'Baron Blud?'

'Just that.'

'Who's Baron Blud?'

'You ought to know. I mentioned him to you once before, and actually tipped you off to keep an eye on him, but apparently you didn't.'

'What makes you think he did this?' enquired Floyd.

'One thing and another. I haven't any definite proof.'

'Then you don't wish to directly accuse him of murder?'

The Knight shook his head.

Floyd sneered: 'You wouldn't just be trying to give me a false trail to follow, would you?'

Lance rose from the bed and walked across to the window. He looked out for a moment, then turned around. 'What do you plan to do about this, Ernie?'

Floyd grated: 'I'd like to take you in and hold you on suspicion.'

'But you're not going to?'

Floyd shook his head. 'No — not if you give me your solemn word you didn't commit this murder.'

'You'd take that?' asked the Knight, mildly surprised. 'I thought you hated my guts.'

'I do. But I know you well enough to know you're not a liar. And what I think of your activities when I'm off duty is different to what I think when I'm on. Bit vague that, but you'll get what I mean. What's more, I fancy you've got something up your sleeve somewhere that only you know about. That right?'

'It may be; and if it is, you can take whatever credit's coming.'

'I'm still waiting for your word, you know. You didn't have anything to do with it, did you?'

The Knight looked him full in the eyes, and Floyd liked the clear honesty of his gaze. There was no deception there; the

Knight was telling the truth, and nothing but.

He said: 'You've got my word I didn't do it, Ernest. And I'm not going to deny it would be rather nasty for me if you took me in. But foist off the hounds of the law for a few days, and I hope to have everything you need in the way of evidence that will convict Blud and send him to the gallows.'

Floyd nodded and turned round to direct the men from the morgue, who had arrived with a stretcher. The body of Costan Dervent was laid upon it, and the procession started. Within fifteen minutes, Lance Knight's rooms were empty again. He breathed a sign of relief and thanked his stars that Floyd had been on the case. Anyone else would have roped him in, bar Floyd. Keen as he was to land the Knight, knew in his own mind this was none of the Knight's doing. He knew quite surely that Lance could never have committed such a clumsy, obvious murder and then gone to the trouble of calling the police. And he was giving the Knight a chance.

So the adventure was going on, and the Knight was going on with it.

* * *

The Knight dined out late that night; and who should he have bumped into but none other than his erstwhile friend, Farlow.

It was a surprise meeting on both sides. Farlow was sitting with his back to the Knight, and neither of them had noticed the other; although later, the Knight remembered he had detected a faint odour of swine about the place. The meeting proper was brought about by a new waiter who was dexterously plying his soup between kitchen and table — or at least, prided himself he was plying it dexterously. But actually he was a very new waiter, and had not obtained the poise and the ability to snatch a laden tray from under a Dowager Duchess's foot without breaking a plate as yet.

It wasn't a Dowager Duchess's foot actually, this time, but it served the purpose. It was Lance Knight's elbow jutting over the back of his chair as he dined in solitary state. And the very new waiter who was plying his soup dexterously suddenly found he wasn't nearly so dexterous after running full tilt into a rock-like elbow.

He whooped involuntarily, the tray spun aloft, and a score of diners watched with fascinated eyes as it seemed to hover stationary in mid-air. Then it descended like manna from heaven, splattering soup on all and sundry, with a fine disregard for rank or station.

Lance himself received only an eyeful; the waiter, becoming extremely dexterous at the last minute, skipped nimbly aside. The tray clattered to the floor, and the vast portion of three bowls of clear soup delivered themselves, bowls and all, upon the benighted bald head of Mr. Sebastian Farlow.

Which was rough luck on Mr. Farlow, because he still had two bruises and one bump where the Knight had already ministered to him. Mr. Farlow roared.

So did the Knight — with laughter. The spectacle of Farlow's already unlovely face peering out through three layers of clear soup and a variety of succulent vegetables was exhilarating in the extreme. Worth, as the Knight said later, 'a damn sight more than any guinea a box!'

Farlow spotted the Knight almost as the Knight spotted him. And he suddenly stopped roaring, and allowed the harassed waiter to mop soup from him with a tray cloth.

'My, my,' said the Knight in accents of deepest shock. 'Stealing soup at your age, Sebby! Aren't you ashamed?'

Farlow snarled, and without speaking left the table for the men's room. The Knight regarded his companion closely. She was young, and seemingly a certain type of woman. He doubted very much if she was anything more to Farlow than the companion of an evening. He rose from his chair, walked across, and deposited himself into a spare chair at the table. The woman looked at him, and the blond-peroxide hair wiggled on her forehead in what she obviously thought was a ladylike gesture of enquiry.

'You don't know me,' said the Knight pleasantly. 'Nor do I know you. But we can put that right. You see this?'

He allowed the end of a fifty-pound note to show in his palm. Her eyes went wide and she nodded.

He said: 'Would you like to earn this?'

'Would I, big boy,' she squeaked in a slate-pencil voice. 'An' how I would. I don't like that bald-headed old moose anyway. Let's you 'n' me blow someplace other than this, what say, hey, honey?'

'You've got me wrong,' he told her with a grin. 'You don't have to do anything for this fifty. Just beat it.'

'Hey?'

'Beat it. B-E-A- . . . '

'Okay, okay, I get it. But I think you're nuts handing round fifties for nothing. I got some lady friends who'd love to meet you, Rockefeller.'

'Some other time,' said the Knight with a grin. 'Now you take hold of this and get going before Egghead comes back. Good night, kid.'

'Swell,' she said, stowing the money in her bag. She looked reflectively at the

Knight and rose to her feet. 'Would you like my telephone number, big boy?'

'No, thanks. I've got a book full of 'em at home. So long.'

She sighed regretfully, and he watched her vanish through the far doors. Then he watched the floor show and awaited Farlow's return. It was almost through before Farlow, sponged down and newly brushed, slithered back through the tables with the apologetic waiter still kneading his sleeve anxiously. He stopped in surprise at the table when he saw the Knight, then looked about for the woman. The waiter looked too.

Knight said: 'All right, Jeeves, you can go. My friend doesn't mind having your excellent soup poured over him, do you Sebby?'

The waiter went, and Farlow rumbled: 'What's this game? What have you done with — with Marjorie?'

'Marjorie? That her name? She's gone, Sebby. But don't get upset about it. You can get them ten-a-penny like her. But you can't get pleasant little chats with me every day, can you?'

'We've got nothing to talk about, Knight,' said Farlow uneasily. 'And I'm leaving now, anyway.'

The Knight leaned over and suddenly gripped Farlow's hand as if he were shaking hands with him after a long absence. It looked like nothing more than a handshake, but beads of sweat stood out on Farlow's forehead, and he almost buckled at the knees.

'Sit down,' intoned the Knight, still smiling agreeably. 'Sit down and let's have a long chat about old times, Sebby my lad.'

Farlow sat down; there was no other choice. And the Knight released his crushed hand and grinned at him affably.

'I expect you'll be wondering why I want to talk to such a low worm like yourself, Sebby, won't you? The truth is, I just can't resist furthering the fun and games a bit and telling you what I think may happen to you one of these mornings. There's no doubt, Sebby, that one of these mornings you'll dodder out to the scaffold, and the hangman will say, 'Lovely morning, isn't it?' and then he'll adjust the noose and make sure he's tied a good knot — a knot that will hit you in the right spot and almost knock your head off your shoulders. I don't know the exact procedure, but probably he'll then permit some member of the clergy to mumble a few words over your immortal soul — if he can find one who'll take the job on. Then they'll all say, 'Well, nice knowing you,' and the platform'll slip away, and the noose will jerk hard up, and your neck . . . do you know what it does to your neck, Sebby? No? Let me elucidate. Have you ever seen a chicken whose neck's been wrung? You have? Good. That's what it does to your neck, then — blue veins, swollen marks, deep bruises . . . and if there's any slip, you kick and kick, and pull the noose tighter . . . '

Farlow's face was clammier than ever; his hands were clenched on his lap. He husked: 'Stop it. You — you can't frighten me.'

'My dear old chap, I'm not trying to. Not at all. Perish the thought. I'm merely looking on the whole thing in a purely academic light, Sebby. But it does happen. It always happens to the ungentlemanly, and you're one of the most ungentlemanly men I ever met.'

Farlow almost whispered: 'I haven't done anything.'

'I think you'd have a hard time convincing the police of that. They already have their eagle eyes on your tame zombie, Blud. You'll probably hang together.'

'They'll never get anything on us. And if they do, I hadn't anything to do with it. I — '

'Go on.'

'You're trying to get information out of me, aren't you? That's your game. Well it won't work.'

The Knight yawned ostentatiously. 'Anyway, I'd advise you to watch your steps. I've already tipped off the police to keep a lynx-like eye on the delightful Baron.'

'They can't . . . he's — '

'Is he? How interesting. Tell me more.'

Farlow had said too much already. He grunted: 'You can do all the funny stuff you want now, Knight. I still say we'll have those plans and that woman within the next few days — perhaps sooner. Then you'll be wiped out.'

'I'll look forward to that,' agreed the Knight. 'What will you use? A barrel of gunpowder? Or will your delicate little pal get busy with another knife?'

'Never mind what we'll use. It'll look like accidental death.'

The Knight smiled pityingly. 'You'd have tried it long ago, wouldn't you, but for those plans? You don't know where they are — haven't the faintest.'

'We'll find out.'

'Will you? Suppose, for instance, that I'd parceled them up, put them in the post, and left them to be called for at a poste-restante address? Feel up to trying every post office in Britain to locate them? Suppose I'd merely checked them into a safety deposit vault at my bank? Or I might have checked them into a left luggage office in any one of fifty stations. I may have done none of those things. They could be hidden beautifully and safely in my own rooms.'

'We won't look for them personally. You'll tell us just where they are.'

'I will? That would be foolish of me, wouldn't it? Almost as foolish as Costan Dervent was not to telephone at once for police protection when you threatened him.'

'I didn't threaten him.'

'Blud, then. You were with him, I know that. I dare say you'd meant to kill him anyway — he was getting too far ahead in his negotiations with Lebania, and the man behind you saw his beautiful oil fields slipping away, didn't he? But when he came round to my place, you saw a chance of killing two birds with one stone. You felt certain I'd be taken in for the murder — but I wasn't, Sebby. And that goes to show that you don't know exactly what the police do know and don't know; so you'd better start worrying.'

'I — I'm not worrying. I don't know anything about any murder.'

The Knight chuckled and studied his fingernails. 'I can imagine Korvin getting into a devilish stew about those plans. I suppose he can't think why he can't find the experimental drillings. I couldn't think why myself until I studied the drawings — and then it all seemed rather a good joke. You'll laugh no end when you know, Sebby.'

Farlow shrugged and stood up.

'Going already?' asked the Knight in mild surprise. 'I was just getting interested in our chat.'

Farlow leaned over the table. 'Knight, I've had orders to make you one last offer: fifty thousand pounds for those plans! I don't think it will do any good to ask you, but there it is, if you've changed your mind.'

'Fifty thousand? When can I collect?'

Farlow sneered: 'You can't collect — not until we have the plans in our hands. You don't think we'd be taken for mugs, like I was last time, do you?'

The Knight shook his head. 'No, I hadn't much hope of that. However, it was worth a try, wasn't it?'

'You refuse the offer?'

'I not only refuse it, but if you don't get out at once I'll plant my size nine behind you.'

Farlow got out at once; the Knight watched him check out his coat and hat and put them on; and noticed with sudden interest that they were not evening clothes, but a motoring outfit — warm leather coat and gauntlets. The Knight whistled, watched Farlow leave the place, then hurried outside after him. He was in time to see Farlow's car swing down the road in the opposite direction to the one his home lay in.

The Knight returned in a thoughtful mood, and ordered his dinner. But before the soup-balancing waiter could bring the first course, he stood up suddenly and walked to the cloakroom, checked out his things. He was worried. That customary premonition of danger was travelling up and down his spine like a charge of high voltage. His scalp tingled with the awareness of something, somewhere, amiss. What, he could not have said; but there was only one thing he could think of.

Janis, alone at Land's End, on that gaunt cliff, with a woman who would stop at nothing to achieve what she wanted . . .

Was anything wrong? Had he been right to trust a job like that to a woman who had always been sheltered and protected? If anything happened to her . . .

He drove the thought from his mind, but he knew that he had to go down and see — make sure she was still there, make sure she still held Marcia Korvin.

He returned to his flat first, to pack an extra gun in case. Then he telephoned the nearest car-hire service, for Janis still had his own Cadillac. They said they could supply him with a fast car, and he hurried from the flat again. A woman who had been standing watching the building suddenly climbed into a waiting taxi — and with a shock of trepidation, he realised that it was Marcia Korvin, or someone damnably like her!

10

In Which a Woman Becomes a Princess

He was aboard the running-board almost
before the car had started moving; and he
said: 'One moment, driver.'

The driver stopped in surprise. The
woman, huddled back in her seat, a mass
of furs, stared haughtily at him.

'Well, well,' said the Knight jocularly,
but with a touch of stress behind the
words, 'the charming dictator's daughter.
How are we this evening?'

She said frostily: 'Driver, drive on. This
man appears to be drunk.'

And for the first time he began to have
doubts; and they were his undoing. For
the driver did as ordered, and shot out
into the traffic. Lance had to skip nimbly
from the running-board to the footpath
before he was crushed against the side of
the car by pressure of traffic. But he saw
her looking back — and he saw the look

of triumph in her eyes! He was sure. Sure it was Marcia Korvin.

And now he was worried, too. Hitherto he had always played his hands alone; but this was different. Here a woman's life hinged on his capabilities, and that was a thought that made him pause. He would have taken any chances with his own life; but he did not have the right to take any chances with the lives of innocent people.

He finally decided it would have to be different this time. And he telephoned Scotland Yard, spending some minutes in conversation with Chief Inspector Floyd. Then he took out the hired car and trod on the gas towards Land's End.

Half an hour after he had left, a large closed car purred silently from the Yard, and took the same direction. And just in front of him, Marcia Korvin, who had changed her taxi for a waiting car, also raced towards the lonely stone cottage.

Thirty miles in front of her, Farlow, as arranged, followed the same route.

And someone else was driving that way, also . . . someone whom Lance was very anxious to meet.

The Knight raced his car along the rocky cliff road, swerved round a precipitous drop — dodging death by a hair's breadth — and ran the car into the shadows of some boulders. He got out and surveyed the lie of the land. If anyone had come here in a car, Farlow or anyone else, they certainly had that car well hidden. The cottage itself stood lonely and desolate atop the cliff a hundred yards away; and without wasting more time, Lance started along the crumbling pathway towards it.

There were no lights in the windows; and a strange eerie air of utter lifelessness pervaded the surroundings of that grey stone erection, below which the seas dashed furiously against the base of the cliff.

Then he saw the door.

It was open slightly. From within came no sound, no sign of life. He smiled grimly to himself. He knew it was a trap, and yet he had to chance it this time, and rely on the plan and its hiding place to gain him time. Time was the vital thing. He must keep anyone who happened to be within that cottage preoccupied.

He had reached the door now, and he stood as if undecided. He pushed it open and called: 'Hello? Hello, Janis?'

No reply.

He stepped cautiously into the interior of the cottage — and felt the thud of a heavy weapon on the back of his neck, sagged at the knees, and fell flat out on the stone floor. He hadn't expected it that quickly, but still he did not lose himself. He fought against the whirling grey tones that flooded his brain, fought and conquered, and knew he would not lose his senses.

Knight was powerless to resist as they lit a lamp and bound him tightly to the chair that had so recently housed Marcia Korvin. He allowed his eye to wander round — and saw Janis.

Janis! His heart ached for her. She was fastened by arms and legs to a number of hooks that had been knocked into the hard mortar between the cracks of the stones. She lay spread-eagled on the floor, a blue bruise above her left eye, and her body scraped and scratched as if she had struggled against it all and been roughly handled.

Farlow had lit an oil lamp, and Blud was caressing a large lump of driftwood with which he had evidently struck the Knight. Marcia Korvin was standing against the far wall, looking coldly dispassionate at the scene before her.

They were all here — a rogues' nest!

The Knight opened the conversation. 'Well, well, well,' he said brightly, although his head was aching infernally, 'I must say it's pleasant to see you again. The three of you, all together, eh? But where's the other? That delightful character who employs you, Mr. Farlow. Aren't we having the pleasure of his company?'

'He's coming,' grunted Farlow. 'And this time he's making sure you hand over those plans.'

'So it was all a plant?' the Knight said as if unable to believe his ears.

'It was,' said Farlow with a grin. 'We thought you'd take the bait. Once you'd seen Marcia Korvin in London, we knew you wouldn't be able to resist rushing down to see what had happened.'

'There was more than that even,' the Knight said brightly. 'I must admit I was suspicious when you rolled out of the club tonight in motoring togs. And when you said Baron Blud was out of town . . . at least, that's what you were going to say, I think. Of course, it's plain enough now, boys. The dear baron was down here preparing this little setup, wasn't he?'

'That's right.' Farlow grinned.

'And now that I've been fool enough to walk into a trap, what are your intentions? I hardly think they'll be honourable, eh?'

'They certainly won't,' said Farlow. 'Far from it. Eventually we intend to kill you. But since we have to get that plan, a spot of refined torture comes first.'

'Nothing Blud did could be refined,' said the Knight, but under his airy badinage was a tenseness, a tautness, and a prayer that everything would run to plan. 'And I may as well tell you now you can stick hot irons or any other pleasant devices on me until my eyeballs drop out, and I won't sing a solitary line.'

Farlow said: 'It isn't you who's going to

be tortured — it's the woman, Princess Janis!'

That stopped Lance; that wasn't according to plan. He hadn't thought of that; he had thought they'd have moved her away. But he said: 'What makes you think that will move me? She means nothing to me. It's her country I'm trying to help.'

'Don't give us that,' sneered Farlow. 'We know damn well you and her think a lot of each other. We've been told.'

'By whom?'

'By the same person who told us where you'd imprisoned Miss Korvin here.'

The Knight tensed. This was it. 'And who was that?'

'It was I,' said a new voice from the door, and into the circle of lamplight stepped Colonel Mercer.

The Knight felt an internal rushing wind in his head; he was completely thrown. He hadn't expected that, above anything.

Mercer! He was the man at the head of the gang. That was why the gang had known where Janis was hidden, where

Count Dornich was staying, and all about the negotiations with Lebania. Of course; it was simple now. The colonel had Janis's complete confidence.

'You're surprised,' said the colonel matter-of-factly. 'I can't say I blame you. But you might have guessed where the leakage was coming from, mightn't you? There was another thing, too. Did it ever strike you as funny that a retired army colonel on half pay could keep up a house and staff like mine? Or did you think I had a private income?

'Well, I had, Mr. Knight. I retired with quite a bit of money. And between us, Mr. Farlow and myself — Mr. Farlow is my cousin, by the way — converted it into a fortune. He handled the business side of it all, and I directed operations.

'And then a man who thought I was a close personal friend of his wrote to tell me he had struck oil, and his country's troubles were over. That was the King of Lazania. I endeavoured to persuade him to sell me shares and let me have concessions, but he regretfully refused me. He said the wells would be for the good of the state, and I knew he meant it. But Korvin, whom I had once met, heard of this, and decided he saw a chance to seize control of the country. I armed his hill bandits and ruffians, and they swooped on the forces of the crown, which were only a mockery, since royalty had always sat firmly on the throne of Lazania.

'They were wiped out and the royal family captured. Princess Janis, who was staying in England at that time, not knowing there was trouble afoot, came to stay with me at my suggestion, for I told her I was afraid she might be assassinated. Actually, I knew by then that Dornich had escaped with the plan, and I knew Janis would be a very useful source of information as to his whereabouts. I think you can guess the rest, can't you? Time is growing short, and the threatened intervention from Lebania is dangerous. If we can produce the plan, and grant concessions to Lebania ourselves, we have won. That is why, although I am not very enthusiastic about having to subject poor Janis to torture, I fear we must. We must have that plan, Mr. Knight, and it is in your power to give it to us. Do that, and I promise you both your deaths will be quick and merciful!'

Janis whispered, looking up: 'Don't — don't give it to him, Lance. They'll do as they please with Lazania if you do.'

Mercer made a sign to Baron Blud, who came forward with his ghastly white face grinning at the helpless woman, took from his pocket a thin piece of solid rubber, and swished it approvingly in the air.

Mercer said: 'Are you ready to speak?'

Lance bit his lip, looking undecided.

Mercer said: 'Perhaps this will help you to decide,' and gave the sign to Blud.

The rubber lashed down savagely across Janis's stomach, and she shrieked in unbearable agony.

Lance bit his lip and called: 'Stop — wait a minute. I'll tell you.' Blud looked disappointed. Lance said: 'There's a door in the far wall. It leads into a cupboard. The keys are in my pocket.'

Mercer got the keys himself. 'You'd

better be right.' He crossed to a long narrow door, set in the wall on the sea side. 'This?'

Lance, only three feet from him, bound to the chair, muttered: 'Yes. It's inside there, in a small box on the floor.'

Mercer stared at him long and hard; then he fitted the key and turned the lock. His hand closed about the knob, and he turned that and began to push . . .

Lance moved. Like a catapulting stone, he hurled forward from his tensed toes, chair and all. He struck Colonel Mercer directly in the small of the back, which forced him sprawling through the door and into the inky night.

The pounding of the surf blended with the colonel's screams into a mad medley of sound. And then he was gone, and nothing but the raucous screeches of the gulls who had been disturbed rose to their ears — that, and the still roaring waves battering fiercely against the multitude of jagged spike-like rocks.

And inside the cottage was silence; disbelief.

The Knight lay where he had fallen,

inches from death himself. Baron Blud stood foolishly staring, the rubber in his hand. Farlow was white and pasty and motionless. Marcia Korvin was tight-lipped.

She was the first to move, and said: 'That simplifies the whole affair.' A gun sprang into her hand. She went on: 'Now we don't really need to give any concessions to you, Farlow. Your boss has gone, and we can arrange for you to go the same way. Blud . . . '

The Baron grinned maliciously and began to advance upon the quavering Farlow. The Knight said in a wild shout: 'This is it, Sebby! Now or never! Take a chance, man!'

His voice must have penetrated into the inner mind of the craven Farlow, for he suddenly bunched up and took a running jump at the Baron. Blud went down under his weight like a log — and Marcia Korvin's gun splattered lead.

Farlow stopped running and fell to his knees. The gun roared again, trium-phantly. Farlow looked mildly amazed that it didn't hurt as much as he had expected, then he flopped down on his face and began to squirm, his squirms gathering violence as the fierce, biting pangs of his stomach wounds grew more intense.

Marcia ignored him and turned to Blud again. 'Now, Baron, we'll proceed with the torture, shall we?'

Blud had regained his feet, and his eyes were darting venom at Janis. He was sore and angry — and he wanted to take it out on somebody.

Marcia looked at the Knight and said: 'You did us a service by disposing of Mercer for us. Now do us another and tell us exactly where we'll find the plans. And make no mistake this time.'

She didn't notice Farlow, who had stopped squirming. She failed to see his hand reaching into his side pocket as he gasped for air, and Baron Blud was too intent on continuing his sadistic rites to bother with a man as good as dead. The first they knew of it was the sharp cracks, two of them, almost on top of one another. And Marcia went down scream-ing, her gun flopping uselessly from her hand. Baron Blud was badly hit, but he retained his balance and walked over towards Farlow, who still lived. Farlow kept on pumping slugs into him — wildly, desperately . . . and he was lucky. Blud was a mere two feet from him when his gaunt frame stiffened abruptly. His eyes glazed. He went out, blood spurting from his forehead.

For a minute, the silence was broken only by the roaring surf, and Farlow's feeble groans. Then there was a rush of steps on the path outside, and Floyd burst in wildly, with four men behind him.

'Come in, Ernest,' the Knight said with a weak grin, 'and see what you can do for Janis Smith. She's fainted.'

The police had arrived as he had asked them to; but if it hadn't been for Farlow, he was afraid they'd have been a little late. They released him, and he went immediately to an old clock standing on the mantelpiece. He removed the back, then forked about round the front of the works. What a pity for Mercer, Farlow, Blud and Marcia Korvin that they hadn't thought of looking for the plans there!

' . . . Today the armies of Lebania walked into Lazania,' said the voice of the BBC newsreader, 'and the Korvinites were completely overwhelmed. The royal family has been released, and mopping up operations are in progress.'

Lance switched off the radio and looked at Janis. She put soft arms about his neck and drew his face down to hers. He said: 'Well, that's the end of Korvin. Poor devil — how was he to know the oil fields had their source in an underground cavern? No wonder he couldn't find them.'

She smiled. 'Are you still in trouble with the police?'

'Didn't I tell you? Farlow made a full statement before he finally died in the hospital. I'm in their good books until the next time, thank heavens.'

There was a moment's silence. Then he said: 'I suppose you'll be casting off Janis Smith now, and going back to Lazania as their Princess?'

She nodded sadly. 'We agreed, Lance.'

He kicked a cushion. 'Oh well, there'll be other adventures for me, somewhere, sometime. I really do wish you luck . . . '

She drew him to her again and whispered: 'But Lance, don't be so anxious to get rid of me. I'm staying here for another fortnight, and if you don't mind I'd like to go on being plain Janis Smith with you for all of it!'

'Mind?' echoed Lance. 'Mind?'

They didn't speak much after that. Much could be said and done. In two weeks — it was a lifetime.

And for once the Knight left adventure to look after itself!

PASSION'S VICTIM

1

June Mallory was seeking a victim. There was something hard and calculating in her eyes as her gaze swept over the crowded tables of the Silent Parrot night club.

She was very well known at the club — these last few weeks she had been a constant visitor. Yet she loathed the place. It looked cheap and nasty. Everywhere the paintwork was faded and drab; there were damp patches on the walls, and in many places the distemper was flaking so that it was the ruination of a dress if one stood too near. Yet for some unknown reason, the Silent Parrot was popular. Society had taken it up. The service charges had leaped to fantastic heights, but that only seemed to make the club more popular. Every night money flowed into the Silent Parrot; and because there was money there, June Mallory was a constant visitor.

It was her job to seek out men and money.

She wished that Emile Gruvel had not accompanied her tonight. Already he had had too much to drink, and drink always made him a very amorous Frenchman. Twice his encircling arm had embarrassed her and she had had to draw away from him. He leaned towards her now, his eyes bright with wine.

'You are the most beautiful of the beautiful,' he said, 'and yet so cold. There is ice in your veins. But I could melt that ice. If you would only let me love you, I would show you the meaning of paradise. Together we would make money — much money — and you would live like a queen.'

His flowery words nauseated her. What an idiot he was! If Lucius knew that he was pestering her with his attentions, there would be the dickens to pay. One word to Lucius and Emile Gruvel would be back in the gutter where he belonged. The only way to get rid of him was to find another companion — to do the thing she had come to do. But it had to be a man with money to spend. A great deal of money.

She disengaged Gruvel's arm, and her eyes searched again. As before, they focused on the man seated in the corner. He was on his own, and somehow he looked right out of place in the Silent Parrot. He made her think of the wide-open spaces; of blue skies and distant snow-capped mountains. Perhaps it was his deeply burned tan — a tan that defied all the efforts of the glaring lights. It was obvious, too, that he wasn't at home in evening dress, although his jacket fitted his broad shoulders with that utter perfection that only Savile Row can produce. He was in no way handsome; his nose was too big and his jaw too heavy. Yet when he smiled at one of the waiters, she had thought it the most likeable face she had ever seen.

She knew she wasn't guessing when she put him down as a man recently home from abroad. That he possessed money was obvious. On his table stood a bottle of the most expensive *vino* supplied by the club. He was interested in her, too.

Many times in the last hour she had caught his gaze fixed upon her. Then why didn't she set machinery in movement for an introduction? Wasn't he the very sort of man she had come here to find? And who would be easier than a returned wanderer? But still she hesitated.

Boyd Vincent was indeed staring at June Mallory. In that overheated atmosphere where all the other women looked like dropping flowers, she was a fair rose. The glory of her hair was matched only by the brightness of her eyes. And her mouth — how could he describe her mouth? It was a mouth designed to sweep some incredibly lucky man into the seventh heaven of ecstatic desire. What was such a lovely woman doing in this sordid dive?

And that dark individual with her. His attentions were obviously annoying her. Given half a chance, he'd take him by the scruff of his neck and kick him off the premises.

A noisy group flowed into the room. Emile Gruvel looked up at their entry and then clicked his tongue against his teeth.

'Ah!' he exclaimed. 'The beautiful Mrs. Swanson. She is one who likes me for myself; and she has the money, too, that Lucius likes. I have not wasted my time in coming here tonight.' Getting to his feet, Emile bowed elaborately. 'I am desolated to leave you. But this is business. One night — soon — there will be no businesss, and then we will talk of love again. But we shall meet later again tonight.' He made his way between the tables, swaying slightly as he walked.

'Thank goodness!' June breathed. 'I'm closer to liking Mrs. Swanson than ever before.'

Her eyes went back to the man in the corner. Yes, he was still staring at her. She had got rid of Emile, so what was she waiting for? Lucius would be pleased if she cultivated the stranger. And she knew how desperately anxious she was to please Lucius. Her gaze went to the clock on the wall and she saw it was almost exactly half an hour after midnight. The time was slipping by. Unless she did something, and did it soon, the whole night would be wasted.

But she didn't look again at the man in the corner. Instead she looked at two men who had been seated together. They had come to their feet as though they were leaving. She decided that neither would serve her purpose. Both were big and burly, and their evening clothes sat uneasily upon them. Those clothes had come off the peg — the wearers wouldn't be wealthy men.

There were two doors leading from the club; and as the two men walked away from their table, they suddenly separated. One went to one door and his companion to the other.

'Everybody will stay where they are!' one of them ordered loudly.

From outside came the shrilling of police whistles. A surge of panic swept through June. It was a police raid, and she had been caught up in it. It was the worst thing that could have happened. And — and she had been getting on so well, too. Lucius would hate that she should become known to the police. He might have nothing more to do with her, and that would be fateful to all her hopes.

In the club, waiters stood foolishly, balancing their trays, as though they had been stricken in mid-stride. Everybody gaped at the two grim figures near the doors. A woman broke the spell by laughing.

'It's a long time since I had my picture in the newspapers,' said Mrs. Swanson.

There were many men and women who seemed alarmed. One woman buried her head in her arms and began to sob. June noticed her wedding ring.

'It's nothing to get upset about,' her companion said, but his mouth was trembling. 'The papers won't print our names. Your husband's not likely to hear about it.'

Without warning, the lights were switched off and the room plunged into darkness. One of the staff must have turned the lights off at the main.

'Don't move!' roared a voice. 'The place is surrounded — none of you can get out.'

Instinctively, June had come to her feet. But what was the use? There was no possibility of escape. If she was caught in the attempt, the police would only take greater notice of her. She mustn't make herself conspicuous in any way.

A hand closed firmly over her fingers. 'This way!' whispered an urgent voice.

She saw only an indistinct shape, but she knew it was the man who had been seated in the corner. It would have been no use even if she had tried to protest. She was almost jerked off her feet and then swept through a doorway. He had dragged her into the kitchen. There was a sudden gasp as he bundled into someone and then swept him unceremoniously aside.

June saw a faint square of light — the kitchen window.

'I came in here some time ago,' said the voice, 'and I remembered the window was wide open. Get on the table and then dive through it.'

She knew it was no use at all. The building was surrounded, and they would be arrested as soon as they appeared in the yard. That would mean a further charge against her, a charge of impeding the police in the execution of their duty. It would probably mean imprisonment, and that would be her finish with Lucius.

But she made no move to protest. There was something in the stranger's voice that had to be obeyed. Onto the table she climbed, and she had no difficulty in getting through the window. He squeezed through after her. It was quite dark, but not so dark that they couldn't see they were standing in a narrow yard that was surrounded by a high wall.

'It's hopeless!' she protested. 'They'll be waiting for us outside.'

Steel-like fingers grasped her arm, and she was dragged forward. 'I'm getting you out of this,' he said. 'Now shut up.'

There were some boxes at the base of the wall, and he climbed on one in order to peep over the top.

'It's an alleyway,' he whispered, and his voice was rich with amused excitement. 'A copper is on guard at the end of it. So I'm going to climb over in that corner and fall right on top of him. As soon as you see me jump, you scramble over and run for it. You'll be all right — you'll see!'

Somehow she knew that she would be

all right. He crossed the yard, and she saw him pick up something from the corner. As she climbed on top of a box, she saw him standing upright against the dark sky, and then he disappeared.

She scrambled on to the wall while her long dress hampered her movements. She dropped and found herself in the alleyway. As far as she could tell, there was no one at the entrance now. She reached the entrance and a startled gasp escaped her. Out of the darkness a large figure had loomed.

'Come on,' said a familiar voice. 'The coast is clear.'

Her hand was seized and she was forced to run. Just outside the entrance, she glimpsed a squirming body.

'It was easy,' said the stranger. 'I found a sack, and when I dropped on the copper, I wrapped it round his face. We'll be in the car before he can get at his whistle.'

Into a side street she was whirled, and here a car was standing. Without any ceremony, he picked her up and flung her inside.

'You — you don't waste much time,' she managed to gasp.

The car swung round two corners in quick succession. He flung back his head and laughed.

'That police raid's the best thing that could have happened,' he told her. 'For days I've been trying to get some excitement out of this old town, and I've succeeded at last. I've really enjoyed the last ten minutes. Besides, I've met you, and that's the most exciting thing yet.'

She scarcely heard the last remark, for she had turned to look through the rear window. The headlights of a following car had flashed through it. But it was only a taxi. She saw it turn into the curb and stop.

No, they weren't being followed. They had got clean away. Lucius would be glad about that.

They merged into the traffic of Piccadilly and then turned into another side street. The car slid to a stop. 'Where are we?' she demanded.

'My flat,' he told her.

'If you don't mind, I'd rather go straight home.'

'Nonsense. That wall wasn't at all clean; we're probably in an appalling state. My man is on duty, and he'll soon fix things for you to get a clean-up. Besides, we must celebrate our escape.'

They entered a modern block of flats, and the liftman stared curiously at June as they were swept upwards. On the third floor they were admitted to a spacious flat by a stickily built little man with the ugliest face June had ever seen.

'We've been doing some steeple-chasing, Tuggy,' the stranger told him. 'Is the bathroom in a fit state to be seen by a lady?'

The little man scowled. 'There's nothing wrong with any bathroom that I looks arter,' he snapped.

The stranger flung open a door. 'It's all yours,' he said to June. 'And, Tuggy, we shall need something to drink. Champagne, whisky, gin . . . ' He gazed enquiringly at June.

'If it's not too much trouble, I'd like nothing better than a cup of tea,' she said.

'You walk straight into Tuggy's heart,' her rescuer said with a smile. 'He prides himself on being the finest tea-maker in the world.'

She grimaced when she saw her face in the bathroom mirror. Her hair was disheveled and there was a black streak down her face. No wonder the liftman had stared at her! Her frock was dirty and crumpled, and she had ruined the toes of her shoes. She cleaned herself up as well as she could and then went back to the sitting-room. There was nothing ostentatious about its furnishings, but every article betokened wealth. Lucius would be pleased with this new friend of hers.

'Tuggy won't be a moment,' he said. 'While we're alone, what about some introducing? I'm Boyd Vincent and I live here with my man, Tuggy Hoskin.'

For some reason his engaging smile made her feel terribly cheap. 'I'm June Mallory,' she said.

He stared at her intently, almost as though he couldn't tear his eyes away. Suddenly he was embarrassed. 'I — I don't know what you'll think of me,' he said then. 'Tuggy and I have been out in the wilds for years and we've only just returned. The sight of a white woman is still a novelty to us — especially a beautiful white woman. I — I mean . . . '

Tuggy entered with the tea tray. June sipped her tea and then she gazed up at the little man. 'It's true, Tuggy,' she said. 'You are the world's best tea-maker.'

'T'aint nothing,' Tuggy growled. But his ugly face beamed.

Both men looked dismayed when, the tea finished, she declared that she must leave. 'It's so terribly late,' she said. 'I had no intention of staying so long at the Silent Parrot — and all the excitement has upset me a little.'

It wasn't true. She wasn't tired and she wasn't in the least upset. She only knew that she must get out of that flat. If she didn't, something might happen that would come between her and Lucius. Nothing in the world must cause that to happen. The sooner she was safe in her own flat, the better.

'But of course,' Boyd Vincent agreed. 'It must have been most upsetting for you. I'll run you home in next to no time.'

'My flat is quite near,' she told him.

He said nothing during the short journey. But when the car had pulled up opposite her front door, he turned to her very seriously. 'I'm probably doing the one thing I shouldn't do,' he said earnestly. 'If so, please forgive me. But I've been away so long I'm a bit lost on etiquette. Everything in London is strange to me. I expected so much on my return; but until tonight, I've only been bored. Meeting you is the most exciting thing that has ever happened to me. I mean that. And having met you, I want to meet you again. It's probably an absurd favour to ask, but could you lunch with me today? Perhaps we could spend the rest of the day together. It's going to be a wonderful day — I'm enough of a weather prophet to know that.'

'Right! I'll come.'

In her own sitting-room, June was amazed at herself. She had almost fled from Boyd Vincent's flat — had fled because she had never wanted to see him again. Now she had promised to lunch with him. She looked at a photograph on the mantelpiece and suddenly her mouth became hard. She was being a fool. Lucius would welcome Boyd Vincent with open arms. It was her greatest chance — she would never have another like it. She dare not let it slip.

She would spend the day with Boyd, and in the evening she would introduce him to Lucius Lee-Stoddard. She dare not let herself become soft now. She had to play Boyd Vincent for a sucker.

Meanwhile, Boyd had driven back to his flat with his head in the clouds. Within a few short hours, he would be lunching with the most wonderful woman in the world.

His dream woman!

2

June got out of bed at midday. As she splashed in her bath she sang softly to herself, and when she looked into her mirror she saw that her eyes were bright with excitement. It was such a wonderful morning that it was good to be alive. That afternoon she was lunching with Boyd Vincent!

What an idiot she was — what a crazy idiot. She was behaving like a schoolgirl just because a man was taking her out to lunch, and she had known him only a matter of hours.

'I'm losing my grip,' she told herself angrily. 'If I let myself go soft now, I'll never have another chance. I've just got to make sure that nothing can go wrong. It mustn't go wrong. As far as he's concerned, I'm only a pick-up woman. He's been away in the wilds so long, he's bound to find any woman exciting. The novelty will wear off; he'll meet other women, and that will be my finish. No, I gave up being foolish years ago. I'll spend the day with him, but tonight he is going to meet Lucius.'

She went into the sitting-room and picked up the photograph she had looked at the night before. It was that of a smiling middle-aged man — a man who looked as though he hadn't a care in the world. Yet June's eyes were full of tears as she gazed at that carefree face.

'I'm not being foolish anymore,' she told the photograph. 'If I play my cards right, it may only be a matter of days now. I told you I would succeed, and I'm going to. Nothing is going to stop me.'

She spent a long time choosing her outfit for the day. But she was ready when her doorbell rang.

Boyd Vincent stood on the threshold. In a light sports jacket with open-necked shirt, he looked even bigger and burlier. Despite herself, June thrilled at the quick admiration that flashed into his eyes at sight of her.

'You take my breath away,' he said. 'I shall be pinching myself all day just to make sure that you really are with me and that I'm not dreaming it.'

They lunched at a tiny restaurant, the excellence of whose cooking was a secret known only to a select few. It was a meal that passed in a flash. June had little to say; she was content to listen to Boyd. It was good to listen to him. He told her of strange and funny happenings abroad, and never once did he bore her. Yet the meal was something of a strain, because all the time her head was fighting a battle with her heart. Her head kept insisting that it would be fatal to let Boyd Vincent interest her too much.

On the pavement outside the restaurant, he paused. 'What now?' he demanded. 'The best part of the day is ahead of us.'

'It's for you to say. You are the returned wanderer.'

'Well, it's a lovely day for the river,' he suggested. 'We can go down to Staines, Henley or any other place you fancy. If we took out a punt, we could just laze about and talk.'

She thrilled at his suggestion of the river. She remembered a lovely holiday she had once spent at Staines in those far-off days when things had been easy and she had known nothing of life's darker side.

'We'll go to Staines,' she decided. 'I shall love it.'

In the car on the journey down, she took her mirror from her handbag. In her eyes she saw the same excitement that had been there that morning. But now she made no effort to fight it.

There was no reason why she should not enjoy every moment of the outing. She liked Boyd's company, and there was no harm in that. For the first time in years, she had a feeling of real happiness, and she wanted to give herself to it heart and soul. It couldn't make any difference to her other plans. That night she would return to normal. She would introduce Boyd to Lucius, and that would be that!

There was no difficulty in hiring a punt. June made herself comfortable on the cushions and, in effortless fashion, Boyd began to pole the flat-bottomed craft upstream.

'This is a perfect setting for you,' he

said once. 'You put all the other river women in the shade.'

She wished she had better control over her heart. It was absurd that the mere sound of his voice should set it leaping.

'You haven't been back long yet,' she said. 'Wait until you meet a few more women. I'll become very ordinary then.'

'Never!' he exploded. 'I shall never notice another woman while you're around.'

They moored the punt at last in a backwater under the shade of drooping willows. June moved over so that he could lie beside her.

'There's nothing in the world quite so good as a real English summer day,' he said. 'It's a shame we get so few of them.'

She looked at his sun-browned face. 'You seem to have spent a lifetime in the sun. And now you can tell me all about yourself. I'm dying of curiosity.'

'I'd sooner you talked about yourself.'

Her heart contracted rather painfully. She didn't want him to know too much about her. Within a few weeks — perhaps days — he would be hating her.

'There's nothing to tell,' she evaded, and hated herself for a catch in her voice. 'My parents were fairly well off and I went to a good school. Business college came next, and I worked for a year or so as a secretary. Then an aunt of mine died and left me a little money. So there's no need for me to work now unless I want to. Now tell me about yourself?'

'That's soon done. I left this country when I was very young, and I've kicked around the world quite a bit. I managed to work my way through an American college and get a mining degree. In a Mexican mining camp I met Tuggy Hoskin, and I persuaded him to go exploring with me. I had certain ideas about a range of mountains I'd seen as a kid. We spent years on those mountains, and I still don't know how I managed to survive. But at last I found what I knew they contained — silver. We staked our claim and got to work, and the El Pesco Silver Mine was the result. A short while ago, Tuggy and I sold out to a syndicate and then came back home.' He laughed boyishly. 'We decided we'd do nothing except spend the rest of our lives enjoying ourselves,' he went on. 'We soon changed our minds about that. Already I'm looking round for some business that will keep me fairly busy.'

'Then Tuggy is rich, too?' she asked archly.

'Rich enough,' he said. 'But all the money in the world won't make any difference to him. He signed on as my servant years ago and he says he's sticking as long as I want him. I guess that'll be for life.'

June remembered reading about the selling of the El Pesco Silver Mine. A tremendous sum of money had been involved. Very nice, too. Now she had found Boyd Vincent, she would be able to introduce him to Lucius. It was the most wonderful stroke of luck that had ever come her way.

For a moment she knew fear. Boyd was staring at her in such a strange way. Surely he had not been able to read her thoughts?

'Maybe I'm crazy,' he said. 'I've spoiled

many things in my life by being too eager. Yesterday I would have said that I had everything in life that I wanted. Today, having met you, I know that I've nothing — just nothing at all.'

'That's just foolishness, Boyd.'

'It's the truth. I know I've no right to say this. You'll say it's too sudden — that I haven't given myself time to think. You'll probably say that love at first sight is something in a storybook — something that can't happen in real life. But it *can* happen. I know that. I fell in love with you the moment I looked up and saw you in the Silent Parrot. You looked so different — so utterly out of place. I knew then that you were going to be the only woman in my life. Then the police came in, and I had a chance to speak to you and to help you. When I left you last night, I knew it was no idle pipe dream; I knew I was in love with you. Now that I've met you, there just can't be any other.'

The expression in his eyes was the most wonderful thing she had ever seen.

'Do you think you might learn to love

me?' he asked. 'Do you think you might — one day — marry me?'

She had no idea that the expression in her eyes was the mirror of that in Boyd's. She had no idea that her lips were slightly parted, as though eager for the kiss that would declare her love. She only knew that her whole being was aglow.

'You — you do care!' he exclaimed, and his voice was the sweetest music in her ears.

His strong arms went around her and her mouth had become one with his. There was nothing she could do about it — she had been swept along by a surge of power that was beyond the control of calculating reason. She kissed Boyd as she had never kissed anyone before, and the ecstasy of it was supreme.

'Oh, June!' he murmured. 'June, my dearest! I still can't believe it. How could you possibly love me? I'm ugly; I'm rough and crude, and I shall never do you justice when we go places together.'

She held his face between her hands and then drew it down to her, kissing him again. 'That is what I think about you,' she said, and snuggled her head into his shoulder.

'I've just got to make this dream come true,' he told her. 'We'll get married — as quickly as we possibly can.'

A tiny hand of fear clutched at her heart. She dare not talk of marriage yet. 'It *is* real. We've found one another, and for the moment we must be content with that. For days — weeks — we shall be discovering new things about one another. It's all going to be so wonderful. And then — then we'll marry.'

She knew she was crazy. She ought never to have let him make love to her. But she couldn't have stopped him. She had wanted his kisses so much.

'Tonight we must celebrate,' Boyd said. 'We'll get back to town as quickly as we can. If I could have my way, I'd let today go on forever.'

'It will go on,' she said, and hated herself for saying it, because that night she intended to introduce Boyd to Lucius Lee-Stoddard. She dare not go back on her resolution. For four years she had prayed for this chance. She must go on

— even if it meant the sacrifice of her newfound love.

They drove back to town, and Boyd left her at her flat so that she could change. Within the hour, he was back and waiting for her. 'You look so wonderful,' he said. 'I'm sure I'm living a dream.'

She kissed him. 'You won't need to pinch yourself now.'

They dined at the Savoy, and Boyd saw to it that the meal was perfection. They stayed a long time over it, too.

'Where do we go from here?' Boyd demanded at last. 'Don't forget the night's all yours.'

June pretended to consider. 'Brain-wave!' she said at last, and she forced a note of excitement into her voice. 'I know the very club.'

His face fell. 'Must it be a club?' he groaned. 'They're such dismal-looking places.'

'Not this one,' she quickly assured him. 'It isn't a real club. It's actually a large house just off Park Lane. Only a very few people know about it, and it's the only place in London where we can really celebrate our engagement.'

'You know best,' he said doubtfully.

They left the car in a street off Park Lane and then walked a few blocks.

'Here we are,' said June, and she stopped outside the wide portico of a large house. The light of a street lamp played full upon it. Into the circle of lamplight a figure came shambling. June saw it and her hand flew to her mouth.

The figure stopped directly in front of Boyd, who found himself staring into the ravaged face of a shabbily dressed man whose deeply sunk eyes appeared to be bright with fever. Before Boyd could guess his intentions the man had reached up and seized the lapels of his jacket.

'So you're her new sucker,' the down-and-out said wildly. 'Haven't you learned yet that she's one of the gang? By the time she gets through with you, you won't have a penny left. She hangs around every bloke who's got money.'

3

Boyd took the thin wrists and forced the clutching fingers away.

'He's crazy!' June exclaimed. 'He's always lounging around here and — '

'You know why,' shrieked the down-at-heel figure. 'It was you who — '

There was the sound of heavy footsteps, and a burly figure came into the circle of lamplight. 'What's going on here?' demanded an official voice.

The figure whirled and at sight of the policeman a startled gasp escaped the pallid lips. Then, whirling again, the man raced off into the darkness.

Boyd stepped in front of the policeman. 'There was no trouble,' he said. 'He was just a beggar.'

'You can't be too careful these days, sir,' said the policeman with a shrug. 'I'll recognise him again if I see him, so I'll keep my eyes open.'

He continued on his beat, and June

realised she was trembling with relief. How terrible that Tony Langdon should have accosted her on this night of all nights!

Boyd took her arm. 'Did you know that man?' he enquired.

'Only very slightly,' June answered. 'He used to run round with some people I knew. He came into money unexpectedly and it went to his head; within a year he'd spent it all. I tried to stop him, and that was all. Since then, he's blamed everybody for his misfortunes except himself.'

Thank goodness that was the truth!

'Of course,' said Boyd, satisfied, 'Do we go in?'

The place was entirely different to the Silent Parrot. They entered a wide hall that might have been that of a millionaire's mansion, and June's wrap and Boyd's coat were taken by a discreet butler. A footman ushered them into an enormous lounge. Two elderly and well-dressed men were talking near the fireplace, but otherwise the room was empty.

'Can I get you something?' enquired the footman.

'Make mine whisky,' June said. She turned to Boyd. 'The club's upstairs. We shall probably find it quite full. If you don't mind waiting a few minutes, I'll go and tidy myself up.'

The footman brought a decanter, soda water and glasses, and indicated that Boyd was to help himself. He also succeeded in making it clear there was no charge.

On leaving the lounge, June had run lightly up the broad staircase. She obviously knew her way about, because on the first floor she pulled aside a heavy length of valuable tapestry. It shielded the opening of a narrow passageway that was only dimly lighted. Down it she walked, turning to the right and again to the right until she came to a door. She tapped on it and waited.

'Come in!' directed a smooth voice.

June hesitated for a moment and then stepped into a luxuriantly furnished office.

'Good evening, Lucius,' she said. 'Have

you been wondering what happened to me?'

The sallow face of the man behind the desk had lighted up at sight of her. He was singularly handsome, and everything about him seemed correct in every detail. Not a hair of his head was out of place, and he might have been poured into his evening clothes. It was only when people studied Lucius Lee-Stoddard closely that they realised some of his features weren't quite so much in keeping as they appeared.

His eyes were too small for his face and his mouth was thin-lipped. Though his face had lighted up, he was regarding June as a beast of prey might regard its victim. But she was smiling, and she appeared to see nothing wrong.

'I've been waiting for you,' he said. 'I know of course that you were with Emile at the Silent Parrot last night. I also know that the police have no knowledge of you. Luckily Emile was with the Swanson crowd and he was bailed out by some of their friends. But tell me, chicken, where did you hide?'

'I didn't hide,' she said. 'There happened to be a he-man just returned from overseas in the Parrot. As soon as the lights went out he seized me, thrust me through the kitchen window, knocked out a policeman before the man knew what was happening, bundled me into his car, took me to his flat, gave me tea, and then took me home.'

'Most interesting,' said Lucius Lee-Stoddard.

'That isn't half of it,' June told him gaily. 'Does the name Boyd Vincent mean anything to you?'

'I can't say it does.'

'Or the El Pesco Silver Mine?'

His brows furrowed. 'Boyd Vincent! I remember now. Isn't that the name of the man who sold the El Pesco Mine?'

'Correct,' she told him. 'He's rolling in money, and he's come back to England to have a good time. I've been with him all day. I spent the afternoon on the river with him, and some hours ago he asked me to marry him. If I agree, he'll marry me tomorrow.'

His eyes narrowed, and he drew in his

lips. The meanness that was his nature was plain to see. 'Of course, you will agree.'

She went round the desk to him. 'Don't be foolish. Why do you force me to be so blatant where you are concerned, Lucius? Years ago you swore you would never trust a woman, but surely you can trust me now; I'm turning down a fortune just because of you. I've brought Boyd Vincent along with me tonight, and he's waiting for me in the lounge now. I've found him, and now I'm turning him over to you. As one of your hostesses, that's my duty, isn't it?'

The smile came back to his lips. 'You force me to trust you, June darling,' he said. 'In fact, I'm going to do more than trust you. It's not this Boyd Vincent you're going to marry, but Lucius Lee-Stoddard. You're coming into the business as my partner in all things. With both of us working together, we shall be on easy street.'

He gathered her into his arms and she went willingly. She gave him her mouth almost as completely as she had given it to Boyd. There was an icy feeling all down her spine, but she knew it didn't mean a thing. If it was the only way, then she would marry Lucius — and she would be glad! As his wife, she couldn't fail to get what she wanted.

After a little while, she forced herself away from him. 'You mustn't keep me,' she said. 'I must go back to the lounge. We mustn't run any risk of losing the biggest fish that's ever come into our net.'

'I'll walk in and meet him presently,' he said. 'Then, when you've a chance, come back to me here. There's a little job I want you to do with Emile tomorrow night — a most important job. I'll tell you all about it when you come back.' He kissed her again.

Outside the door, as she restored her lipstick, the blood was thudding in her temples. It was success at last. On the next night she was to help Emile on a job. She had won their confidence. Her mission would soon be ended!

Boyd was just finishing his second whisky when she returned to the lounge. 'I'm so sorry,' she said. 'I met someone I knew and they kept me talking. We'll go straight up now.'

She had been right in declaring they would find plenty of people on the floor above. As she piloted Boyd inside, she wondered what he would think of it.

He took it in at a glance, and knew it for a high-class gambling den at once. He began wondering why June had brought him here. At the back of his mind was the niggling memory of their encounter with the down-and-out. It persisted even though he tried to shut it out altogether.

There were several card schools, and in one corner an intense group were seated round a poker table. But the centre of attraction appeared to be a roulette wheel.

'I adore roulette!' June exclaimed, and she didn't realise how artificial her voice sounded. 'And my luck is bound to be good on such a wonderful day as this.'

She pushed her way to the front and then she began to stake heavily. Watching her, Boyd wondered about her resources. Again he remembered that encounter outside. June's money wouldn't last long either, if she flung it away in this reckless manner.

But June knew she had nothing to worry about. It was Lucius's money she was playing with. Her plunges would encourage other people to gamble heavily, too. She lost time after time and then received all her money back in one tremendous win.

'I knew it!' she said. 'I knew I couldn't lose.' She turned gaily to Boyd then. 'Come and share my luck,' she invited. 'It's no fun just looking on.'

Boyd began to wager as recklessly as she had done. He lost, and he went on losing. It seemed the celebration of his engagement was going to be an expensive one.

A voice suddenly sounded behind June. 'Good evening, Miss Mallory,' a man said. 'How nice to see you here again after all this long time. I really began to think we had offended you.'

She turned to see Lucius. 'Good evening, Lucius,' she greeted. 'I've been looking out for you. I want you to meet my friend, Mr. Boyd Vincent.'

Boyd turned to the proprietor. He was the type of smooth gambler he had seen at work all over the globe. It was funny how the breed always ran true to type, and it hurt him that June was familiar with men of this stamp.

'I am delighted to know you,' Lucius said. 'Any friend of Miss Mallory's is a friend of mine. Perhaps I may look forward to seeing you often.'

'You will,' June assured him. 'Boyd is just back from the wilds. I've an idea he'll soon be showing us what real gambling is like.'

'Perhaps later you will join me in a drink, Mr. Vincent.'

'Thank you,' said Boyd.

He turned back to the table. He doubled his stake, and again it was raked away. The gambling fever had seized him.

Presently June touched his arm. 'I'll give my luck time to change,' she said. 'But you go on playing. I'm going downstairs for a few moments. I'll have a few more bets after that, and then we'll think about leaving.'

Boyd went on playing recklessly. He

had gambled many times in his life, and had gambled wildly, too, so he knew how the excitement of it could grip. But there was no feeling of excitement tonight. The evening that had started so wonderfully was really being wasted. If only they could have gone somewhere else! Why did she have to bring him to this place?

June was away a long time. He turned away from the roulette table and then stood to watch the poker school. The size of the stakes made him blink. The gamblers who came here certainly played with real money.

He began to watch the dealer. He was a thin-faced, hook-nosed man whose pale eyes never blinked. In front of him stood a small fortune. Watching closely, Boyd became sure that the man was cheating — that he knew the value of every card he dealt.

Boyd had known card sharps out in the west of America; some of them had shown him their tricks. Yes, this man was a card sharp right enough. He was cheating on behalf of the house. It hurt more than ever that June should be familiar with men like Lucius Lee-Stoddard.

He found the atmosphere suddenly stifling. If only June would return. He needed fresh air badly. Looking around him, he saw that all the windows were heavily curtained. He could stop behind one of them and open a window if necessary.

He crossed to the nearest curtain without anybody noticing him. He pulled it aside and received a shock. The curtain did not mask a window — it masked the opening of a narrow passage. He let the curtain fall behind him, wondering if he should venture down the passage in search of fresh air. As he did so, the door at the end opened and June and Lucius Lee-Stoddard stood revealed. Some instinct caused Boyd to remain perfectly still.

'You'll be quite safe with Emile,' Lee-Stoddard was telling June. 'Nobody takes any notice of a man and woman in a car late at night, but a car driven by a single man sometimes causes suspicion. Now, don't forget your instructions. You must catch the last train from Charing Cross tomorrow, and Emile will have the car waiting for you at Purley Station.'

'I shan't forget,' June said.

Boyd's nails suddenly dug into the palms of his hands. Lucius Lee-Stoddard had taken June into his arms. 'Goodnight, my darling,' he said.

June clung to Lucius, and she kissed him just as she had kissed Boyd on the river that afternoon. Lucius closed the door and Boyd was alone in the passage.

How he held himself in check, he never afterwards knew. The urge came upon him to go into that room and strangle Lee-Stoddard with his bare hands. This was the end of all of his dreams. That afternoon he had been at the very summit of happiness — and all because he had given his love blindly. Well, the blinkers had been taken off now. June Mallory was part and parcel of this gambling setup. A cheap and nasty little crook!

4

When June returned to the gambling room, she saw Boyd still at the roulette table. 'I seem fated to meet people tonight,' she said. 'This is the second time I've kept you waiting.'

He moved away from the table. 'I've gambled enough for one night,' he said abruptly. 'D'you mind if we leave now?'

'But you've lost so much money,' she objected. 'You can't let Lucius get away with all of it. You must try and win some of it back.'

'We can come again tomorrow or some other night,' he said tersely. 'Maybe I've been too long in the wilds. I don't seem to get used to this sort of atmosphere. You'll have to give me time, June.' He used her name with difficulty.

'Of course.' She nodded. 'We've had rather a hectic day, haven't we? It has been such a wonderful time and so many wonderful things have happened.'

'Yes,' he said with an effort. 'A wonderful and most surprising day.'

Boyd grimly drove her straight back to her flat. She was still so excited that his silence made no impression on her. At the moment only one thought was in her mind — she was now a real member of the gang. Next evening she was going to do a job with Emile.

At the door of her flat she invited Boyd in, but he shook his head. 'You're much too tired,' he said. 'Do I see you tomorrow?'

Her face filled with concern. 'That's impossible. I'll be out all day and most of the evening. But we could lunch together the day afterwards.'

'Right. I'll call for you.'

She kissed him, but not as she had kissed him on the river, and he hated the fact that her kiss still thrilled him. Only a short while ago she had been kissing Lucius Lee-Stoddard more passionately than she was kissing Boyd now.

If things had been otherwise, June would have realised that something was wrong. But no sooner had she closed the door than she ran to her sitting-room. She took down the photograph from the mantelpiece. 'It won't be long now,' she said to the photograph. 'Only a matter of weeks. I'm bound to succeed. It's taken me such a long time, but soon . . . soon we'll be together again.'

Despite her excuse to Boyd, June did not venture out next day. It was nearly eleven o'clock at night when she left the flat and took a bus to Charing Cross. She caught the last Purley train with plenty of time to spare. At the station she waited until most of the late home-goers had gone. She was the last to walk out of the subway. Outside, in the station approach, a car was standing. Emile stepped out to open the door for her.

'It is good we are together,' he greeted her in his flowery way. 'It is what I have always waited for.'

She hoped that he wasn't going to prove difficult. But surely he wouldn't dare — not when he was out on a job.

The car turned into the Brighton Road, and once they were through Coulsdon, Emile's foot went down hard on the accelerator. Into Redhill they raced, and then he slowed to turn into a side road. Presently the car was crawling, and Emile was obviously looking for something. The headlights picked up a signpost whose solitary arm pointed down a lane.

'This is it,' he said.

He drove a little way past the signpost, and then the car bumped onto the grass verge. He switched off engine and lights, and gave a sigh of satisfaction.

June's voice was anxious as she asked: 'What exactly have we come here for, Emile?'

'Didn't Lucius tell you?' he demanded thickly.

'It's the Waketon Castle job, isn't it?' she asked.

'It is. Soon, my pigeon, we shall be carrying a fortune in the back of the car. When it is safe in Lucius's possession, we shall have much money to spend, you and I.'

'But — but why do we have to pick it up here?'

'The police would like to know the answer to that,' he chuckled. 'But I will tell you. The Waketon Castle burglary was the biggest in years. The stuff was so hot that our friend the burglar did not dare to carry it far. So he hid it out in the country. Having done so, he told Lucius all about it, and they made a deal. Lucius never allows anyone he buys from to visit him, and that is why we are here. Soon a car will come down this road, and in that car will be the burglar. He will stop and ask us if he is on the right road. While he is doing that, he will place a bag in the back of the car and then go on. We will wait a few minutes, and then we shall head back to London by a different way. Simple, isn't it?'

His arm crept along the back of her seat.

'We may have some time to wait,' he went on, his voice growing thicker. 'There is no reason why we should waste time. It is the plan that if any stranger comes along, we should pretend to be a spooning couple.'

'Well, there isn't going to be any spooning,' June retorted. 'You've got to keep your wits about you.'

'All I ask is one little kiss.'

But she knew that to let him kiss her once would be fatal. If that happened she would have real trouble on her hands, quite apart from the fact that his mere touch offended her.

'There is something you should know, Emile,' she said quickly. 'Lucius asked me to marry him this afternoon. It's the truth,' she assured him. 'And you know what Lucius would do now if I told him you had forced me to kiss you.'

He muttered savagely under his breath. 'Lucius is not in love,' he said then. 'To him there is only power and money. But to me, love is everything. Only with me would you be happy. And why should Lucius know? One kiss, little pigeon, and you shall taste the delights of paradise. Only one, and . . . '

His arm tightened round her shoulders, and he pulled her towards him. Then the lights of an approaching car dazzled them.

'Look out!' she exclaimed. 'We mustn't be seen struggling.'

His arm still imprisoned her. She

forced herself to relax, and she wondered if the oncoming car was a police patrol. If so, and if it stopped, then she might have to kiss Emile in real earnest. She must play the part that had been given her. A shudder ran through her.

Then she thought of Boyd. How wonderful it had been lying in his arms! She had wanted to go on kissing him forever. Perhaps now she would never again know happiness as she had known yesterday.

The car pulled up; it did not look like a police car. An indistinct figure climbed out and crossed the road.

'Sorry to butt in,' said the man's voice, 'but can you tell me if I'm on the right road to Redhill?'

There was a slight thud as something dropped into the back of the car.

'Keep straight on,' Emile said over June's head. 'Turn left at the main road.'

'Thank you,' said the other, and he went back to his car. It had been as easy as that. The car drove on and the sound of it died away in the distance.

Emile still held June close. His hand

cupped itself round her chin, and his face came close to hers. She fought him with her fists. She dare not let him kiss her. She knew now that he had been drinking heavily — probably he had sought courage so that he could bend her to his will. His eyes were aflame with desire. One kiss and the situation might be beyond her control.

'Why should I care for Lucius?' he grated. 'Why should he take you from me? All these weeks I have wanted you. And what Emile wants, he takes.'

'Not likely,' she snapped. 'I'm going to travel in the back. You'll let me get, out or else — '

She wrenched herself free of his arm, and then she heard a shot which was so near that she felt that her eardrums had been shattered. Emile jerked upright in his seat and fell forward across the wheel.

Some strange instinct made her move quickly away from that curiously twitching body. As she did so, there was another shot, and then a searing pain in her right arm. Instinct inspired by fear made her lurch forward just as Emile had done.

There was movement in the back of the car, which swayed as someone jumped out. Running footsteps followed, and June opened her eyes to see a vague shape disappear into the darkness.

She looked down at Emile and saw that he was dead. Horror flowed through her veins. Like a madwoman, she scrambled out of the car and ran up the road. She didn't know where she was going — she only knew she must get away from the car where the mysterious assailant had been hiding.

Suddenly she screamed wildly. Out of the darkness a figure had materialised.

'What's wrong, June?' said a familiar voice.

She must be already mad. It — it couldn't be true that out of the darkness had come the one man in the world whom she wanted most.

But it was! She was being held in Boyd Vincent's arms.

5

Boyd's anxious face was staring down at her. 'I heard the shots and I came running,' he said. 'What happened?'

She clung to him. 'There was someone in the back of the car,' she gasped. 'I — I was struggling with Emile when there was a shot. Emile fell over the wheel, and then there was another shot. It hurt my arm. Then I saw a figure running down the road. I — I was too frightened to move. But — but when I did — I saw that Emile was dead. I couldn't stand the horror of it. Somebody had tried to murder both of us.'

Gently he soothed her. 'Nothing is going to harm you now,' he said. 'I'll get you away from here, and . . . '

Another figure came running out of the darkness. 'What's going on, Boyd?' demanded Tuggy Hoskins.

'June has been hurt,' Boyd said. 'Somebody tried to murder her. The car is just down the road, and there's a dead man in it. Make sure about him, will you, Tuggy? Don't touch anything if you can help it; and if he really is dead, come back here double-quick.'

June remembered something important. 'There's a bag in the back of the car,' she said. 'We must take it with us. If we leave it, the police will find it, and it may give them a clue that will lead to me.'

That wasn't the truth. She wanted Lucius to have the bag. If she could save it for him, he would trust her more than ever; and when he fully trusted her, he was bound to tell her things — things she must know.

'Bring it back with you,' Boyd told Tuggy.

Tuggy hurried off. June held out her injured arm for Boyd to see. A low whistle escaped him.

'You've had a very narrow escape,' he said. 'The bullet passed between your body and your arm, and it's only grazed the skin of your arm.' Carefully he bandaged it with his handkerchief.

Tuggy, carrying a heavy suitcase, came

walking back through the gloom. 'As dead as a doornail,' he announced. 'This was the only bag in the car, and I'm thinking we'd better get away from here as quickly as possible. It's a lonely spot, but the sound of shots travels very far at night. We don't want to face a murder rap.'

June began to shiver. Every moment was precious now. She had been struggling with Emile when he'd been shot — there might be signs of the struggle in the car. Probably some strands of her hair would be clinging to his coat. If the police found her upon the scene, they might put their own construction on the crime and accuse her of murder.

Boyd's car was some distance up the road. He climbed into the back after her, and Tuggy slid behind the wheel.

'Back to the flat,' Boyd said. 'As quickly as you can make it.'

Tuggy headed for the Brighton Road.

June snuggled into the warmth of Body's shoulder, and she felt his arm tighten round her. 'How did you happen to be here?' she asked. 'Meeting you was like a miracle.'

'We'll talk about it at the flat. There's a lot of explaining to be done. You've had a bad fright, my darling, so just lie there and relax.'

At the moment that was all she wanted to do. She knew there must be some explanations; she knew that this murder would upset all her plans. But she didn't want to think yet. At the moment she was content just to be with Boyd. No harm could come to her when she was with him.

The car entered London, and soon they were near the West End. Suddenly Boyd leaned forward.

'Not the front door,' he told Tuggy. 'Drive straight to the garage.'

'Why?' demanded Tuggy.

'June's dress is covered in blood. She mustn't be seen by anyone like that. We'll go up the fire escape and you can force the window for us.'

Luck was with them. Nobody saw them leave the car and climb the escape. Once they were inside, Tuggy lost no time in brewing tea.

'We can talk afterwards,' Boyd said.

It was strong tea, and it put new life into June. 'I'm all right now,' she said. 'I'll tell you everything that happened.'

Boyd insisted on bandaging her arm properly. 'I'll do the explaining for the moment,' he said.

Soon June was staring at him, wide-eyed, while he told her how he had seen her in Lucius's arms the night before.

'I was in a pretty bad state when I came back here last night,' he said. 'At first I didn't quite know what to think. I thought of our day on the river, and I knew it was the real June I had held in my arms then. So I decided that something was wrong — that you were in trouble. Well, knowing that the Frenchman was meeting you in Purley tonight, I decided to be on the spot in case you needed help. Tuggy and I tailed you all the way.' Boyd frowned in puzzlement. 'By the way, what's in this suitcase we lugged out of the car?'

'Among other things, Lucius Lee-Stoddard is a receiver of stolen goods,' she explained with a sigh. 'You'll remember that, some week or so ago,

Waketon Castle was burgled and many priceless articles were stolen. The thief hid the swag in the country and then made a deal with Lucius. Emile and I were sent to collect the swag.' She explained how it had been collected, and how some unknown person had shot at them. 'He — he must have been in the car all the time,' she said. 'I saw him as he ran into the darkness. I'm sure the murderer was Tony Langdon.'

Boyd remembered the fever-filled eyes of the man who had stopped him outside the gambling hall. 'Yes,' he said quietly, 'it all fits in. It must have been a murder of vengeance. It obviously wasn't done by someone who was after the Waketon Castle jewels. He wouldn't have left the suitcase behind otherwise.' He came and sat on the edge of June's chair. 'You haven't told me the half of it yet,' he said. 'How — and why — did you get mixed up with the Lee-Stoddard gang?'

'Well, it happened while I was still at school,' she said quietly. 'One day I was sent for, and I was told that my father had been arrested, tried, and sentenced to fifteen years in jail.' She was twisting a tiny handkerchief in her fingers. 'Father had been chief cashier with a big firm. He was a great friend of the managing director's, and I know he was looking forward to going on the board of directors. One night the firm's offices were burgled and the safe opened by someone who possessed a key. The nightwatchman came on the scene; there was a fight, and the watchman was so badly injured that he was taken to hospital. For a time it was thought he would die. When he recovered consciousness, he swore it was my father he had discovered rifling the safe. Father's books were examined, and it was found that many of the entries had been falsified. Thousands of pounds were missing. I should tell you that my father was very fond of walking at night — he loved pottering round London's old streets. It was proved that he had been out on the night of the burglary, but nobody had seen him so he had no alibi. It was terrible.'

Boyd's arm went round her shoulders.

'I saw Father in prison,' June went on.

'I've seen him regularly since. But on my first visit, I knew he would never live fifteen years. Prison was killing him. Every time I see him now he looks worse. At first there was little I could do. I had to earn my own living. Then I received my legacy. I gave up my job and devoted all my time to the task of proving Father's innocence. There was one man in the firm whom Father had suspected — a man called Gerald Kemp. I set enquiry agents to work, and they finally discovered he had changed his name to Lee-Stoddard, and that he was presumably a wealthy man. I lost no time in getting to know him, and I quickly discovered something else. Sam Wallis, the night-watchman who was so badly injured, is now working for Lucius. He is his chauffeur and general bodyguard.'

'Ah!' said Boyd and Tuggy in unison.

'I became friendly with Kemp,' June went on. 'I even let him put his arms around me. Yesterday he asked me to marry him. I was prepared to do even that because I knew sooner or later he would talk — would let something slip. As soon as I had proof, I intended to turn him over to the police.'

Boyd's arm tightened around her shoulders.

'Thank goodness I came back to the old country when I did,' he said. 'The mere thought of you being married to a man like Stoddard makes me go cold.'

'Don't you worry anymore,' Tuggy told her. 'Boyd and I will take over now.'

'But we mustn't let him suspect anything,' June said. 'Already he must be wondering why Emile and I haven't come back. I must ring him up and tell him I have the suitcase.'

'No!' Boyd said sternly. 'You aren't getting in touch with Stoddard tonight. You'll spend the night here.'

'Here?' queried June. 'Must I?'

'Of course. We've plenty of room. You can't go home with blood on your clothes. You must give Tuggy your keys and tell him what clothes you want — something with long sleeves to cover that bandage. Tuggy will get into your flat without being seen. Meantime, the suitcase will stay here. Tomorrow you'll go to Stoddard and tell him about the murder. Don't say anything about Tony Langdon — let him think that Emile was murdered because of the swag. You'll also tell him you hid in some woods all night and that you caught one of the early trains from Redhill. After that, Tuggy and I will take over — and as sure as my name is Boyd Vincent, we'll get your father out of prison.'

June laughed in sheer relief. No longer was she carrying the terrible burden on her own shoulders. Boyd was going to prove her father's innocence.

Tuggy took her keys and set out for her flat, taking a list of the things she wanted. Then, for a long time, she lay in Boyd's arms.

'Tell me,' he said suddenly, 'does Stoddard always live in that house in Mayfair?'

'Not always,' she answered. 'He's got a big place near Sedly village. Most of his weekends are spent there.'

'And Wallis, the chauffeur?'

'He's usually at Sedly during the summer.'

'Good! It couldn't be better. I've already got some bright ideas about Mr. Wallis. I shouldn't be at all surprised if he isn't the man who's going to put Stoddard in your father's place.'

Meanwhile, Tuggy had entered June's flat; and as far as he knew, he had not been seen. He hadn't reckoned, however, with a watcher who was lurking in front of the block. This man saw him enter, saw the light go on in June's flat, and later saw Tuggy leave. Then he followed.

An hour later, the unknown watcher was speaking to Lucius Lee-Stoddard over a private telephone wire.

6

June went to bed but didn't sleep. She couldn't black out the memory of the night's horrors. First she had to deal with Emile. She had been terrified when she had realised he was determined to make love to her, and then in a flash he was lying across the wheel — dead.

Tony Langdon had murdered him. Poor Tony, whose mind had become crazed and twisted since he had gambled all his money away.

Tony had intended to kill her, too.

She thought of Boyd, and the horrors of the night faded. Even though he had seen her in Lucius's arms, he had still believed in her. There wasn't another man in the whole wide world who was his equal. He was her man — the mate who had been destined for her from the beginning of time.

A tap at the door broke her thoughts, and Tuggy came in with a steaming cup of tea. 'I didn't want to wake you up, miss,' he said, 'but the guv'nor insisted. He says you mustn't be too late leaving here.'

In the sitting room, Boyd was waiting for her. He showed no sign at all of the night's stress and strain. Joyously he held out his arms to her when she entered. 'How wonderful to be greeting you so early in the day, darling.' he said.

June kissed him as though she never intended to let him go again. To think she had almost made up her mind to marry Lucius Lee-Stoddard! She could never have gone through with it. Now, with Boyd to help her, her worries were nearly at an end. Her father would be released from prison, and in a few weeks she would be Mrs. Boyd Vincent.

'You must leave here early,' Boyd told her. 'There's nothing in the paper yet about Emile's murder, but the afternoon editions are sure to carry it. The chances are that Stoddard already knows, and that he's wondering what's happened to you and the swag. So, as you are supposed to have caught an early train from Redhill, you must go to him at once. Your story is quite a simple one. An attempt was made to kill the two of you from the back of the car. Maybe you fainted. Anyway, when you came to, Emile was dead and the suitcase missing. You hid in the woods, you caught an early train, you went home to change your clothes, and you've hurried to him as quickly as possible.'

June suddenly had a premonition of terrible danger. 'I'm almost scared,' she confessed. 'The thought of going to that house — the thought of seeing Lucius — terrifies me. I — I'm so afraid I shall give myself away, and . . . '

Boyd reached over and took her hand. 'You've nothing to worry about,' he assured her. 'There's no reason for Stoddard to suspect your story. And, my dear, your father's liberty may depend on the way you go on playing your part. Tuggy and I aren't going to be idle. We're going down to Sedly village today,' Boyd explained, 'and we hope to have an interview with Wallis, the ex-night-watchman. Your name won't come into it in any way, so there'll be no danger for you. By tonight we'll maybe have discovered lots of interesting things.'

Tuggy was smiling. 'I'll say! The guv'nor and I can be most persuasive. This Wallis guy won't be keeping much back from us — I can promise you that.'

But anxiety was again in June's eyes when she stood outside the Lee-Stoddard house. Would she be able to tell her story convincingly? She must!

'I'm not going to let you down now, Daddy,' she murmured as she rang the bell. She saw the quick look of relief that flashed into the butler's eyes at sight of her.

'You're to go straight up, Miss Mallory,' he said. 'Those are my orders.'

She came to the door of Lucius's office, but this time there was no hesitation. She knocked and went straight in.

Lucius was seated behind his desk. At first glance he appeared to be the same as usual — perfectly correct and perfectly at his ease. But his face was more sallow than ever, and his lips were so drawn in that his mouth was the merest slit.

Lucius Lee-Stoddard — alias Gerald Kemp — frowned at her. 'So you managed to get away?'

She walked quickly across the room and leaned over his desk, trying hard not to let him see that she was afraid of him.

'I know that neither Emile nor you went to your homes last night,' he went on. 'I know, too, that Emile's dead body has been found in the car and that a certain suitcase is missing. The account of the murder will be in the papers at any moment.'

June clasped her hands together. 'Oh, Lucius, it — it was all so dreadful!' she gasped.

Then she told the story in which Boyd had rehearsed her. She told how they had received the swag and how the other car had driven away. They had waited a little while, and then a shot had come from the back of the car. There had been another shot; her arm was suddenly paralysed by pain and she had fainted. When her senses had returned, she was alone in the car with a dead man, and the suitcase was missing. She told how she had fled, how she had spent the night in the woods, and how she had returned to London that morning.

Lucius made no comment, but sat staring at her. Then, slowly, he opened a drawer of the desk and took out a revolver with a long barrel — a revolver that had a silencer attached. He placed it on the desk in front of him.

June's blood turned to ice in her veins. Something had gone wrong — he didn't believe her story.

At that moment, a cupboard door behind him suddenly swung open. June saw that it was a false cupboard, and that it masked a dark opening to another passage. Out of this 'cupboard' stepped Sam Wallis, the ex-night-watchman. It was the first time June had seen him at close quarters since her visits to her father's office. She noticed his beady eyes and his low, brutal forehead, and the thought came to her that Boyd and Tuggy would be wasting their time going down to Sedly village that day.

Lucius Lee-Stoddard made a gesture

and Wallis came to stand at the side of the desk — within arm's reach of June.

'And now,' Stoddard said, 'I have some explaining to do. I waited here last night for Emile and you to return. You failed to do so and I became anxious. Fearing something had gone wrong, I sent a man to your flat with instructions to wait outside if you had not come back. I reckoned that if things had gone wrong, it might be impossible for you to come direct to me.'

'Well . . . ?'

'Well, you didn't come to your flat last night,' he went on, 'but somebody else did. The man — a low type — opened the door with a key and came out carrying a case. He was followed back to the flat of a certain Boyd Vincent — a man you brought here two nights ago. My guard was curious so he climbed a fire escape. He found he could see into Vincent's flat and he was surprised to see you there. He noticed that your clothes appeared to be stained with blood, and he also saw something else — a certain suitcase standing in a corner.'

June fought to keep up her bluff. There was murder in Lucius's eyes. If she failed to convince him . . .

At that moment Wallis spoke, his voice cracking with excitement. 'Who is this woman, boss?' he demanded.

'She calls herself June Mallory,' Lucius said. 'For some time she has been working for me as a pigeon-catcher — a finder of men with money who like to gamble. Why do you ask?'

'Well, boss, it's nearly five years since I saw her last. But I've got a good memory for faces and I don't make no mistakes. Her name ain't Mallory at all. She's June Milford — that's who she is. Old Frank Milford's daughter!'

'Thank you, Sam,' said Lucius. 'It's a good thing I telephoned you early this morning and asked you to come into town.'

'It's her all right,' Wallis insisted. 'June Milford, that's who.'

'Yes,' said June challengingly to Lucius. 'I'm Frank Milford's daughter — the daughter of the man who went to prison in your place. Now you know.'

Lucius laughed. 'So that's the reason you came here; that's why you let me make love to you!'

June knew she had to get away quickly. Feverishly, she looked around for some means of escape.

Lee-Stoddard moved nearer to her. 'First of all, I want the truth about last night,' he said. 'What exactly happened at Redhill? Did you murder Emile? And who is this Boyd Vincent — where does he fit in? Now quit stalling, Miss Milford. I want the truth.'

Why shouldn't she tell the truth? After all, both Boyd and Tuggy knew she was visiting the house. She would tell him they were waiting for her outside. Then he'd think twice before he harmed her. If she played for time, there'd be a chance of escape, and . . .

'Very well,' she said. 'I'll tell you what really happened.'

Just then, a voice barked from the open 'cupboard': 'Hands up!'

Such relief swept through June that her knees threatened to give way. She thought that in her very hour of need, the police had become wise to Lucius Lee-Stoddard: they had chosen this hour to raid the house. She felt that her life had been saved by a miracle. But only for a moment did she feel that relief.

Stoddard wheeled round and Wallis jerked towards the door. Slowly their hands went up. But as Stoddard turned, June saw the man in the doorway. It was Tony Langdon — the man who had tried to murder her in Emile's car! His clothes were caked with dried mud, and the brightness of madness was in his eyes.

'You ruined me, Stoddard,' he burst out. 'You cheated me of every penny. I swore I'd get you and everyone connected with you. I got two of your sort last night, and — '

At that moment he saw June. His jaw dropped and his eyes became livid with fear, as he half-lowered his gun. 'You!' he moaned. 'But — but you — you were killed last night. You — you died with Gruvel.'

There was a dull 'plop' of a report from Lucius's silenced revolver. At the sound of it, the gun fell from Tony Langdon's fingers and his hands flew to his chest. Blood-flecked foam appeared on his lips. He staggered, then for a moment stared wildly at Lee-Stoddard.

'You won't escape,' he gasped. 'I've failed — but — the hangman will get you!'

June started to scream for help.

Lee-Stoddard dropped his smoking gun. 'Stop her!' he shouted.

Wallis's brutal fist swung and knocked June into unconsciousness.

When she came round, she found she was tied to a chair and that a gag had been fixed round her mouth. Tony Langdon's body was still on the floor, and the two men were standing near the desk. Her brain was swimming, but she forced herself to concentrate on what Lee-Stoddard was saying.

'I can't afford to run any more risks, Sam. I still don't know what the woman has done, or who this bloke Boyd Vincent may be. There's a risk he may be connected with the police, and when they get hold of anything they're apt to swoop without warning.'

'I — I don't like it either, boss,' Sam stammered.

'Well, there's no need to panic,' Lee-Stoddard told him flatly. 'I've always been prepared for a quick getaway. Now what are we going to do about this darned body?'

Wallis shuddered. 'I'll leave that to you, boss.'

'You'll drag it out to the back,' Lee-Stoddard ordered him, 'and you'll stick it in a sack. Then you'll put it in the car boot. Drive straight down to Sedly and collect the two suitcases from my wardrobe. They're already packed, and they contain everything I shall need in the shape of clothes and money. Then I want you to drive down to the yacht. But time your arrival for after dark. Carry the body on board, and when we're well at sea we can dump it overboard.'

Wallis looked down at the body and hesitated. 'I — I don't like it, boss,' he said. 'I — '

Lee-Stoddard swore at him. 'You fool!' he burst out. 'You're mixed up in this as much as I am. If the police catch up with us, they'll see that you hang as well as me. Jump to it, man.'

Wallis seized Tony Langdon's feet. He dragged the body into the 'cupboard,' shutting the door behind him.

Lucius turned to June, who quickly closed her eyes as though she was still unconscious. A stinging slap suddenly rocked her head and forced her to cry out. 'I thought that would wake you up,' Lucius grunted. He stood looking at her with gloating eyes, his right hand still open, ready to strike again. 'Soon we shall be leaving here. Yes, we are going away, you and I. My yacht is waiting, and we shall be on the seas tonight. For the next month or so, we shall see something of foreign countries.'

He bent near to her, and she noticed how his fingers were crooked as though they were claws. 'I shall have plenty of time to devote to you,' he went on. 'At the moment you think you hate me. It's nothing, my dear; a mere nothing to the way you're going to love me after we've been together a few weeks.'

He started to laugh with the madness of long-thwarted emotion as he advanced towards her.

7

Boyd and Tuggy went into conference as soon as June had left.

'Tuggy,' Boyd said, 'I think you've worked this out the right way.'

Tuggy grinned and nodded. 'I think so. One or two things seemed fishy: first the bloke who Miss June's father suspected changes his name, and next he blossoms out as a blooming millionaire.'

'Right!' Boyd agreed.

'But the biggest pointer of all is this man Wallis. Remember him, boss? He's the night-watchman who's supposed to have caught Miss June's father at the office safe. It's more than strange he should be working for the other man now.'

'That's a point I don't quite understand. We have to remember that Wallis was so badly hurt that he nearly died. That doesn't sound as though he just received a friendly tap from an accomplice.'

'No,' admitted Tuggy, 'but something may have gone wrong.'

'That's what we've got to find out.'

Tuggy grinned again. 'How do we tackle him, boss?'

Boyd's face became hard and set. 'We're not going to lose a moment over him if we can help it. I'm too worried about June. The sooner I can get her away from Stoddard, the better. If Wallis has anything to confess, then it's got to be forced out of him. We've no time for kid-glove methods, Tuggy. It's got to be direct action.'

Tuggy stood up and flexed his muscles. 'My sentiments entirely. What's the scheme?'

Boyd explained, and Tuggy's eyes widened with delight.

'What are we waiting for?' he demanded at the end. 'Let's get cracking on the job.'

Before leaving London, Boyd obtained the key of a certain deserted warehouse, and here he visited the basement. Then, with Tuggy seated alongside him, he headed for Sedly. It was a nerve-racking drive, and there were times when Tuggy's hair stood on end like iron filings on a magnet.

'I should say we've broken all records,' he commented as they ran into the narrow village street.

They parked the car outside the village inn. Boyd called for liquid refreshment and then chatted with the landlord.

'That reminds me,' he said after a while, 'I believe a pal of mine lives around here somewhere. I'd like to meet him again. His name's Sam Wallis.'

'Ah yes,' the innkeeper said. 'Never a day passes but he comes in here. He's chauffeur to Mr. Lee-Stoddard up at the big house. But I reckon you're going to be unlucky today.'

'Why?' demanded Boyd.

'Sam went up to town early this morning. They tell me Mr. Lee-Stoddard rang through for him early this morning. He may be away for days.'

Boyd and Tuggy exchanged glances. This was indeed bad luck. If Sam Wallis was at the house near Park Lane, it might be impossible to make contact with him.

Boyd ordered another couple of beers.

'We'll go up to the house and make enquiries,' he said. 'We must find out if Wallis is expected to be away some time. If so, we'll have to get back to London double-quick.'

Tuggy pulled a wry face. 'Not as quick as we came down, guv'nor, please,' he pleaded. 'My nerves won't stand it.'

The innkeeper put two tankards of beer on the bar and then looked up as a car roared through the village. 'You're luck's in, gents. That's Sam Wallis who just drove by. Reckon Mr. Lee-Stoddard didn't keep him very long in town.'

Boyd and Tuggy sank their beers in one gulp. 'Come on,' Boyd said. He fairly hurled the car through the village, and they were in time to see a car turn through a gateway at the end of a long drive.

'What now?' Tuggy demanded.

Boyd stopped his car on the grass verge. 'We're going after him. We'll get him at the garage if we hurry. We won't go up the drive — we'll go over the wall!'

They climbed the wall and found themselves in dense shrubbery. Beyond was a stretch of lawn and then a large country house. There was no sign of a car standing in front of it.

'We'll work round to the back,' Boyd said.

They reached the back of the house without being seen, and there was the car, standing outside the back door; but there was no sign of Wallis.

'He's left the engine running,' Tuggy said. 'Looks as though he's planning a quick exit.'

'We'll get as close as we can,' snapped Boyd. 'Something tells me there's going to be a spot of action.'

A full ten minutes went by. Then the chauffeur reappeared, carrying two heavy suitcases. He placed them on the ground alongside the car and swung open the back door. He lifted in one case and then he swung in the other. As he placed it on the floor, something hard and round pressed itself into the small of his back.

'We're from Scotland Yard and we hold warrants for your arrest,' Boyd bluffed. 'Get into the back of the car and don't try to start any trouble.'

Sam Wallis nearly dropped with shock. Pretending to be a detective was the best thing Boyd could have done, because all the time, Wallis had been dreadfully conscious of the dead body in the boot of the car. He had been feeling very uneasy, and his collar had tightened — like a hangman's noose.

Numbly, with Boyd's revolver in his back, he never even turned his head but stumbled into the car just as he had been told. Boyd got in after him and slammed the door shut.

Tuggy climbed in behind the steering wheel and the big car slid forward. No outcry of any sort was raised. Sam Wallis had been kidnapped in broad daylight and nobody knew anything about it. Luck had, for once, been kind to Boyd and Tuggy.

The car swung into the roadway before Sam Wallis turned an ashen face to Boyd. 'You — you're making a mistake,' he sniveled. 'I — I ain't done nothing.'

'Quiet!' Boyd barked at him. 'You get plenty of time to talk later on.'

Wallis subsided. Not another word escaped him during the long ride back to London. In fact he sat hunched up as though he was too afraid to move. The car pulled up at last, and Boyd ordered Wallis to get out. The latter alighted and found himself in a narrow yard, facing a pair of heavy doors which Tuggy was now opening. The place looked like a warehouse.

Sudden suspicion flamed into Wallis's eyes. 'This ain't no police station,' he rasped. 'What are you trying to spring on me?'

Boyd thrust the gun into his ribs again. 'Get inside,' he rapped. 'This is only our first call before going to the police station. You'll see plenty of real police soon enough, my lad.'

He pushed Wallis down the basement steps at the point of a gun. As they passed through the doorway, he switched on a light to reveal that the place was empty except for one solitary chair.

'Sit down!' Boyd ordered.

Wallis glowered at him. 'You ain't a cop!' he accused. 'This is a frame-up: it ain't legal. I got good influential friends, I have, and if — '

'Sit down!'

Sam Wallis sat down.

Boyd waited for Tuggy to appear. He had given him instructions to look for the two suitcases. The minutes ticked by and then Tuggy appeared. His face looked slightly green.

'We've butted into more than we expected, guv'nor,' he gasped. 'Judging from the contents of those two suitcases, Stoddard was all set for a getaway. I don't wonder at it either. I thought I'd have a look inside the boot, and I discovered a queer-shaped bundle inside. I slit it open and I found myself looking at the face of a dead man. It wasn't a pretty sight.'

Wallis began to rock himself in the chair. 'I didn't do it,' he moaned. 'It was nothing to do with me. It — it was the boss who killed him.'

Boyd turned to Tuggy. 'Keep an eye on him. I'd better see for myself.'

His face was grave when he came back. 'It's the poor youngster who shot Gruvel last night — Tony Langdon,' he said. 'It seems Stoddard is in trouble right up to his neck now. Well, first things first. Let's make sure of our Sam.'

They tied Sam Wallis to the chair, and Boyd stood over him. 'Don't keep anything back,' he snapped. 'It's your only chance of escaping a rope round your neck. Well, how did the body get into the boot?'

Wallis's nerve was gone. He told the story right from the beginning, including Lucius's treatment of June.

'What does Lucius intend to do to her?' Boyd demanded fiercely. His expression was so terrible that Wallis would have cringed if it hadn't been for the tight cords.

'He — he's taking her with him,' he mumbled. 'Taking her to the yacht. Then — well, heaven help her!'

Tuggy stepped towards the door. 'We can leave him. The sooner we get to this yacht . . . '

Boyd shook his head. 'That's what I feel — action. But we've got to use common sense. It'll only take us another few minutes to finish what we came to do.

This whole business must be cleared up today.'

He turned back to Wallis. 'Now,' he barked, 'you'll tell me the truth about what happened that night you were supposed to have found Miss Milford's father robbing his employers.'

Wallis's eyes filled with cunning. 'Everybody knows that story. I told it all in court years ago.'

It was evident he thought he was in trouble enough — that he wasn't getting into further trouble if he could help it.

'Tuggy,' said Boyd, 'he's not going to play ball. He needs quick persuasion. See what you can do about it.'

Tuggy rolled up his sleeves. 'I didn't spend half a lifetime in the Mexican backwoods without learning a few things,' he said.

Tuggy went to work. Wallis resisted at first, but at the end of five minutes he was whimpering for mercy. 'Stop it,' he howled. 'I'll tell yer everything.'

'Make it snappy,' ordered Boyd. 'If you try to lie, we'll really get to work on you.'

Wallis ran a tongue over his dry lips. 'It

was Kemp who put me up to it,' he mumbled. 'I was in trouble and I needed money badly. Kemp was frightened — he thought old Milford was getting suspicious that he was faking the books. It was an easy setup, too. Kemp had made an impression of one of the safe keys so he could open it easily. The idea was that I was to come across him in the act, that he was to knock me down, and that I was to identify old Milford as the burglar afterwards.'

'But you were nearly killed,' Boyd said.

'I know, darn it! That wasn't in the contract. He only intended to bash me about a bit. But he hit me too hard. I tripped over a ledger, and I nearly knocked my brains out on a corner of the safe as I fell. But it worked out all right in the end — made it more convincing. And then, well, Kemp had to give me a job afterwards and I became his chauffeur.'

Boyd turned to Tuggy. 'That's all we want to know. Make sure he's safe so we can come back and collect him later on. Our next interview is with this man Kemp. And if he's so much as laid a finger on June, heaven help him!'

8

After Lucius Lee-Stoddard had threatened June, he left her to herself. Sometime later, she looked up to see the butler. She hadn't heard him come into the room. He bowed politely as though she was still an honoured guest.

'I've brought you something to drink, Miss Mallory,' he said. 'It will put new life into you. Pray permit me to help you.'

She let him lift the glass to her lips. Thirstily, she gulped down the fiery contents. She hadn't realised from the dryness of her throat that her thirst was almost overpowering. But, as she drained the glass, the liquor left a bitter taste behind it.

'There — there's something in it,' she said wildly. 'You — you're drugging me. I feel . . .'

'Nonsense,' the butler retorted, no longer polite. 'I should warn you not to create a scene, Miss Mallory. My instructions are to gag you if you cause any kind of an outcry.'

She knew there was nothing she could do. Everything became confused. Vaguely she remembered men coming into the room and untying her. Her legs were too weak to support her and she could not use her voice. They had to carry her from the room.

Later she realised she was lying in the back of a car with Lucius Lee-Stoddard at the wheel, and still she couldn't move. Half-conscious, she became aware of the roar of the sea, and someone helping her up a swaying gangplank. Then she was lying in what seemed to be a bunk in a dark cabin.

She discovered that she could open her mouth — that she could speak again. She could use her limbs too. So she was no longer tied! Perhaps if she tried, she could get out of the cabin. The ship was still tied up — she would have known if it was underway by the motion. If only she could get on shore!

She dropped her legs to the floor and tried to stand, and fell back on the bunk again. It was too soon yet — she wasn't strong enough. But in another ten minutes or so . . .

A key turned in the lock, the door opened, and the light clicked on. Lucius Lee-Stoddard paced into the cabin and closed the door behind him. The light half-blinded June; but even so, she saw he was carrying a short-handled whip.

'So,' he said, 'my prisoner is beginning to recover.' He advanced as she cowered back. 'The sooner your strength returns, the better I shall be pleased,' he said with smooth menace. 'You have a very great debt to repay, and you cannot repay it in full unless you are strong in body and mind. I don't want the kisses of a weakling.'

'You beast!'

He chuckled. 'You asked for such treatment. After all, you dared to pit your wits against mine. But I was to blame in the first place; I was too sure of myself. I should have been careful to have kept an eye on old Frank Milford's daughter. Well, you were pretty smart. Having changed your name, you came to me and tried to get my confidence. You poor little fool! Did you really think I should ever tell the truth about your father? You would even have married me to find out, wouldn't you? What a wasted sacrifice!'

He ran the long leash of the whip through his fingers.

'Now I can tell you everything you want to know,' he went on. 'You see, I no longer have anything to fear. It was a case of either I went to prison or your father went in my place. Naturally I preferred that it should be your father. I falsified his books and robbed the safe, and the only mistake I made was in nearly killing Sam Wallis. Though it wasn't a mistake, really; it clinched the case against your father as far as the jury was concerned.'

His smile faded and two bright spots of red appeared in his sallow cheeks.

'I might still have been safe,' he went on, 'if it hadn't been for you. The killing of that young fool Langdon was nothing — I could easily have covered that up. But you had brought in men to watch me — this Boyd Vincent and maybe others. I don't know what they've found out about me, and that's why I must leave England for a while. But you are going to tell me all that I want to know.'

'I'll see you in blazes first, Lucius!'

'Obstinate, eh? Well, I have my own methods of finding out what I want to know, as you shall see.'

He dropped the whip on the cabin table and then stepped towards her. She tried to rise and jump away from him, but her legs were too weak. He caught her by the shoulders and then pulled her arms above her head. Something snapped round her wrists. He propelled her forward and then stretched her arms to the uttermost. With her toes only just touching the floor, she was suspended from a hook in the ceiling that had once held a hanging cabin lamp.

'I told you I had a lot of time to devote to you,' he said softly. 'You shall suffer until you tell me everything.'

She sank her teeth into her lower lip. Something swished through the air, and every nerve in her body shuddered. But no blow landed. He had only tested out the whip that time.

It swished again. This time it cut deep into her flesh, and she wanted to scream with agony. But she was still biting her lip. How long could she hold out before unconsciousness came?

The whip fell again. Despite herself, a cry escaped her. Lee-Stoddard chuckled, thinking that her spirit was breaking. He prepared to wield the whip again, but suddenly dropped his arm as a rattle sounded behind him. The cabin door burst open. June gave a shout of utter relief. She saw framed in the doorway a huge athletic figure clad in a chauffeur's uniform. It was Boyd!

He took in the terrible scene at one glance. Madly he propelled himself towards Lucius. One moment Lee-Stoddard had his back to June; the next he was flying across the room to smash against the opposite wall with a force that threatened to send him right into the next cabin.

Then Boyd turned tenderly to June. He cut her down and carried her to the door.

'Tuggy is outside,' he said. 'Stay with him, darling. I've a spot of unfinished business to clear up.' He made for the door as Tuggy walked in.

'Everything is going to be all right,' Tuggy told her cheerfully. 'Just leave everything to the boss.' He led her to the foot of a small companionway. Meanwhile, a tornado seemed to be wrecking the cabin behind her.

'Good old guv'nor,' chuckled Tuggy. 'What wouldn't I give to be in his shoes now! But he's got the first right to do some classy bashing, and I will say . . . '

Tuggy was interrupted by the staccato retort of a gun. June's hand flew to her mouth and she gazed, wide-eyed, at Tuggy. He looked blank.

'I guess it'll be all right,' he said doubtfully.

The uproar started again.

'Won't the crew try to rush us?' June asked.

'There's only half a dozen of them,' Tuggy said. 'I followed the guv'nor down and I told them I was from Scotland Yard. I don't think they'll butt in.'

Suddenly the noise stopped. Footsteps approached the door. June felt Tuggy grow tense and saw him point the gun in a new direction. Who was coming out of the door? Loved one — or fiend?

Slowly the door opened, and she flung herself into Boyd's arms. 'Boyd! Darling!'

Boyd hugged her passionately. Then, realising there was still some business to be done, he turned to Tuggy. 'We're taking Lucius out to the car — what's left of him. You follow behind us, June.'

They carried Lucius's battered body out of the cabin. On the deck, a group of muttering men was gathered.

'Lee-Stoddard is under arrest on a murder charge,' Tuggy told them. 'I advise you to stay on board until the police take over. None of you have anything to fear.'

On the journey back to London, June sat in the front of the car alongside Boyd. Several times she touched his sleeve just to make sure he was there.

Tuggy sat in the back with the unconscious Lee-Stoddard, and it was Tuggy who later took June to Boyd's flat because Boyd insisted that he was capable of handing over both Lee-Stoddard and

Wallis to the police by himself.

'June has had a very bad time,' Boyd said. 'She mustn't be left alone.'

They had to wait an hour for him. But when Boyd came in, he was smiling. 'You'll be wanting to know how I managed to gatecrash the scene at the psychological moment,' he told June. 'Well, I took Wallis's uniform. I thought it would help me to get on the yacht if the crew thought I was Wallis. You see, they would know that Stoddard was expecting him. But the crew weren't mixed up at all in Stoddard's criminal schemes; and when Tuggy told them he was from Scotland Yard, they were like lambs. And . . . well, you know the rest.'

Her face glowed with love and admiration. 'How did the gang react to the police just now?'

'Wallis was in a state of terror and he made a clean breast of everything. He told about Langdon's murder and he cleared your father's name. More importantly, I've arranged that nobody will ever know you were in the car when Gruvel was killed.'

Boyd held June tightly in his arms. 'Darling,' he said, 'if it weren't for one thing, we'd get married tomorrow. But I have decided to wait until your father can walk down the aisle with you and give you away.'

'Oh, Boyd,' she whispered. 'That will make it the perfect wedding.'

Tuggy came into the room, grinned, and then went back to the kitchen to make a cup of tea.

We do hope that you have enjoyed reading this large print book.

Did you know that all of our titles are available for purchase?

We publish a wide range of high quality large print books including:
Romances, Mysteries, Classics
General Fiction
Non Fiction and Westerns

Special interest titles available in large print are:
The Little Oxford Dictionary
Music Book, Song Book
Hymn Book, Service Book

Also available from us courtesy of Oxford University Press:
Young Readers' Dictionary
(large print edition)
Young Readers' Thesaurus
(large print edition)

For further information or a free brochure, please contact us at:
Ulverscroft Large Print Books Ltd.,
The Green, Bradgate Road, Anstey,
Leicester, LE7 7FU, England.
Tel: (00 44) **0116 236 4325**
Fax: (00 44) **0116 234 0205**

WHO IS JACQUELINE?

Victor Rousseau

After following a lone husky on the street, Paul Hewlett encounters the dog's owner — a beautiful young woman in furs, who is then savagely set upon by two strangers who attempt to abduct her. Thanks to Paul and the faithful hound, the would-be kidnappers are repelled, and he takes the mysterious woman — Jacqueline — to his apartment, leaving her there to sleep. But on returning, he discovers a grisly tableau: Jacqueline clutching a blood-stained knife, with a dead man at her feet . . .

THE NIGHTMARE MURDERS

Gerald Verner

Following a strange compulsion, Robert Harcourt finds himself consulting a fortune teller who gives him a sinister message. He says he sees Robert in a mansion, surrounded by happy faces. There is a woman, a beautiful woman. Robert is attracted to her, but hurts her cruelly, and so deeply that she will never forgive him. That very night, as the clock strikes the hour of midnight, Robert will take the life of a man dear to her. He will become — *a murderer!*

THE TIPSTER

Gerald Verner

A mysterious man. calling himself 'the Tipster' telephones the *Daily Clarion* newspaper and announces his intention to commit five murders, beginning with Lord Latimer, Senior Steward of the Jockey Club. John Tully, News Editor of the *Daily Clarion*, believes the call to be a hoax by a madman — until Lord Latimer is shot dead while walking in the grounds of his house at Newbury. Superintendent Budd of Scotland Yard is called to investigate; but his powers are put to the test as several more people are brutally murdered . . .

THE MISSING SCHOOLGIRL

Shelley Smith

A schoolgirl goes missing after speaking to a strange man. A jilted painter sets out to take revenge on his rival in both love and art. A room to let harbours a macabre secret. A man fears his soul has been stolen. A woman is haunted by visions of a lost child. An antiques dealer happens across a crook who has previously defrauded him. A foster child has a peculiar obsession with an old painting ... Seven stories of crime, fear, and the mysterious workings of the mind.

THE MISTRESS OF EVIL

V. J. Banis

John Hamilton travels to the Carpathian Mountains in Romania, along with his wife Victoria and her sister Carolyn, to research the risk of earthquakes in the area. The government provides lodgings for them in the ancient Castle Drakul. Upon investigating a disused basement room, the trio discover a skeleton in a coffin with a wooden stake through its rib cage — and Carolyn feels a strange compulsion to goad John into removing it. Soon afterward, a sinister visitor arrives at the castle — claiming to be a descendant of the original Count Drakul . . .